AFTERNOON DELIGHT
BOOK THREE

A COLLECTION OF SHORT ROMANCES

TIMA SMITH

amarok books

AFTERNOON DELIGHT
BOOK THREE

Copyright © 2014 Tima Smith
tima@writingsite.com

Cover design and art © 2015   Lynita Shimizu
lynita@shimizuwoodcuts.com

amarok books
ISBN: 978-1-944932-17-6

AFTERNOON DELIGHT
BOOK THREE

STORIES

SEPARATE VACATIONS

Someday I'm going to get a chance to do this all again, I tell myself, kicking his sneakers, his running shorts, his T-shirt across the bedroom floor toward the closet. I believe that. I do. Reincarnation. I give the T-shirt one final kick and it flies up, just missing the lampshade and catching on the branch of the avocado tree. It hangs there like a droopy flag, swaying up and down, making me even madder.

Except next time I'm going to come back knowing everything I know now. I pick the shirt off the avocado branch, drop it in the closet, on top of the shorts and sneakers. And knowing everything I know now, I'm coming back as a nun.

I slam the closet door, open it, slam it again. It doesn't make me feel all that much better.

I go into the hall, past the bathroom, where wisps of steam are poking out from under the door where the threshold came unglued, fell apart, and hasn't been fixed yet. I can hear the shower going full, then the squeak of the handle as Tuck shuts it off. The shower curtain slats across the rod and I hurry a little down the hall and toward the kitchen. Yesterday I'd have gone in. Yesterday I'd have dried his back. Yesterday he'd have hugged me, wrapped his cook, clean-smelling arms around me and crooned "Lizzy, Lizzy," against my hair.

But that was yesterday.

I open the refrigerator and look inside. I always go for food when I get mad. Like the time Tuck didn't show up for his birthday dinner, even though he was only stopping off for one little drink with his friends. By the time he came home at half-past midnight, I'd eaten fifteen stuffed mushrooms, all the lobster out of the Newburg sauce, and a double-chocolate cake all by myself.

But the things I'm looking at in the fridge aren't going to make me feel any better — yogurt, cottage cheese, celery, fruit salad. The only things I've been eating so I could knock Tuck's socks off in my new bikini.

I shut the door hard and the ceramic bowls on top of the fridge wobble and clink. The little turtle magnet that holds the list I've been working on slides down the door. Linen. Old plaid blanket for beach. E-reader. Sun block. Hammock. I turn away. Oooh, I wish I could kill him.

I look at the calendar hanging near the door, a big red circle around the last two weeks of August. I drew fourteen smiley faces with a yellow magic marker, one inside every day of those two weeks. Just the sight of them makes my eyes go hot and stingy.

The bathroom door opens and Tuck's feet slap the bard hall floor toward the bedroom.

This is *my* summer. *My* vacation. *My* turn to say where we're going and what we're doing. That's the agreement. Ever since our honeymoon, which turned out to be practically the worst two weeks of my life. Up there on top of Wildcat Mountain with more mosquitoes and spiders and snakes than I ever knew existed.

"Our marriage is over," I told him, all scrunched up under the tarp he'd rigged because the little summer shower he'd said not to worry about was still going on after three days. I actually cried into my tea, which already had a big, black gnat floating in it.

"But Lizzy," he said, "it's only eight days old. How can it be over? We haven't even had our first fight."

"Well, get ready," I said, pouring my tea and the gnat into a puddle near my feet. "You don't need me."

"I want you," he said. "I married you, Lizzy. 'Cause you drive me wild." Then he smiled, and even through the drizzle I could see that look in his eyes.

"Let's go to a motel," I said, trying to appeal to that look.

"Just till it stops raining," he said.

"Till everything dries out," I said.

He nodded. "Okay."

That was our first compromise. The Wildcat Mountain Compromise, we called it. And we've been pretty good at kind of thing ever since. Like deciding to switch off vacations. One summer we go where I want, the next where he wants, even if it's white water rafting or camping in the Rockies with bears and wolves. Because while I'm holding onto the side of the raft for dear life or lying there at night listening to huge animals snuffle around the tent, I can always squeeze my eyes shut and think: Next summer is mine. Next summer is mine. Next summer is mine.

And then this morning he goes and treats the whole thing like it wasn't some sacred contract at all but some silly arrangement that just happened to fall out of the sky. Something one of us can break just by saying so. Like it's nothing. Like it's just a matter of handing me my morning coffee and saying, "Hey, Liz, how about this. How about you going off to the beach like you've been planning, and me, well, maybe I'll take off with Max and John D. for some high-mountain camping. Because it's a really great trip they're going on and now Dodge can't go and you wouldn't mind, would you, Lizzy? Would you, honeybun?"

Now he comes into the kitchen. "Think I'll go out and get a meatball sub," he says. Wanna come?" He says it as though everything is hunky-dory. As though he has no idea whatsoever that two hours ago he made an absolutely major assault on our relationship. "You're already skinny enough to fit through a keyhole," he says. "C'mon. You can have a steak and cheese. With lots of onions." He smiles. As though one smile and an offer of more calories than I've eaten in one whole week will make everything just fine.

I turn back to the refrigerator. "No, thank you." I take out a cup of vanilla yogurt.

"Uh, you upset?"

He's such a genius.

"Me?" I say, taking a spoon out of the drawer. "Upset? Whatever gave you that idea?"

He doesn't say anything for a minute. His Nikes shuffle back and forth across the tile. "You don't want me going, do you," he says.

I stir my yogurt.

"Okay, okay. So I won't go. Even if it is the best camping trip that's ever been planned. I'll go to the beach with you for two weeks."

I can sense something's starting to work him up.

"And go right out of my tree," he says.

I put down my yogurt. I can't believe he's said that. "I can't believe you just said that," I tell him. "As if spending two weeks every other year doing what *I* want to do is just too much to ask."

He bangs one fist softly against his open hand, looks at me, stands there and opens both hands toward me as if surely I can understand what's so perfectly clear to *him*. "It's all I get, Lizzy," he says. "Two weeks out of fifty-two to do what I want. Except me, I only get two out of a hundred and four."

I feel my face going red. "And what about *me*? Doesn't the same arithmetic apply? And you know very well how I feel about rock climbing and canoeing and wild animals and sleeping in a tent. But I never suggested *I* wouldn't go, did I? I never said, 'I don't feel like swatting mosquitoes this year so I think I'll do Club Med alone instead.' "

"Just because you're a better sufferer than me," he says, "doesn't mean we have to keep doing it. You hate climbing mountains. I hate sand. We're together all year. Why can't we take separate vacations once in a while?" He leans toward me. "I can't just lay on a beach for two weeks."

As if he's ever done that. He hops up every two minutes. Worse than a kid. Just when I'm nice and comfortable, he wants to go for a jog or get a hot dog or go for a swim. Two summers ago he rented one of those metal detectors, and the only time I saw him for three days was when he passed the blanket working his way down to the other end of the beach.

"I hate that family of seven that always parks themselves two feet away, with five kids who do nothing but squawk and run back and forth kicking sand and fighting over whose turn it is to use the rubber raft. And the teenagers on the other side of our blanket who have four different Pandora stations playing all at the same time. I don't like burning three layers of skin off my back. I don't like the smell at low tide. And maybe I'm crazy, but I think long walks on the beach are just plain boring."

I give him a long look. "Of course, *I'm* most happy when we're tracking deer," I say. "Especially when my legs go to sleep from squatting in one position for way too long because making one move will scare off the deer we've been following since 5 A.M. And what makes me even *more* happy are the five million chigger bites, even though I loaded myself with five gallons of so-called guaranteed protection!"

I can feel myself getting a little out of control. "And what makes me *truly* happy," I tell him, "is discovering that the tree I'm leaning against is covered not with ivy, but *poison* ivy, and then looking down to see a *gigantic black hairy* spider disappearing up my sleeve! I don't like the woods, Tuck. I don't like sleeping on the ground even if there's a space-age cellular mat between it and me that's supposed to give me a night's sleep as comfy as if I was in my own bed. Because it doesn't!"

We look at each other. And the four feet between us feels more like four hundred.

"I'm going to get my meatball sub," he says.

"Good," I say.

He slams the door.

I take three more cups of yogurt out of the fridge, along with the cottage cheese, a dish of sliced peaches, two apples, an orange, and a grapefruit. I carry it all to the table and eat my lunch.

***

"Hurricane's going to miss us."

"I open my eyes and squint up at Nathan, who's been following me around for almost a whole week now, as if just because I'm here alone I must be available.

"Hurricane?" I say, even though I know that one word will encourage him to sit down in the sand beside my blanket and chat at me for at least an hour. I make a point to stay away from radios and TVs when I'm on vacation. I don't want anything intruding from *that* world, because *that's* what I'm getting away from. Although I have to admit that a hurricane is probably something I might want to know about.

"Yeah," Nathan says. "I tried to find you yesterday to tell you."

Yesterday, I hiked three miles down the beach just so he couldn't find me.

"My folks were talking about clearing out," he says. He shades his eyes with one hand and looks out across the water. "I was going to stay," he says. "You know, ride it out."

Nathan's nineteen. He always tries to make it sound as though his parents have come to the beach with him instead of the other way around.

"But now they're saying it was a false alarm and it's going to miss us by a hundred miles." He shrugs. "I was kinda looking forward to it."

"That's because you're crazy," I say.

He smiles. He takes everything as a compliment.

"Will it hit someplace else?" I ask.

He shakes his head. "It's going out to sea."

"That's good," I say, "because as I told you, my husband is off on a camping trip and I wouldn't want him to run into a hurricane." I mention Tuck a lot when Nathan's around, but it doesn't seem to do any good.

"I saw a cyclone once," he says. I close my eyes. He starts to tell me about the cyclone, and I start to think up reasons why I really have to go, but then Nathan's mother comes to the rescue.

"Nathan," she yells. "Nathan!"

He ignores her.

"Nathan!" This time her voice cracks a little.

He sighs. "Guess I better go see what the problem is." He gets up. "Be right back." He comes right back, kicks the sand a little with his heel. "I have to take them someplace," he says. "Probably won't be back until tomorrow sometime." He says it as though he's apologizing. As if we had a date or something.

"Bye," I say.

"Yeah, 'bye." And then he's gone.

I sit up, look down the sand to the water. It's steely gray and flat-looking, like the sky. My skin goes bumpy as a damp wind comes across the beach. It picks up little specks of sand that go in my eyes and mouth. Wouldn't you know that right in the middle of my vacation the weather would go bad.

I look around the beach. Even the public part is mostly empty. Everyone but me knew it was going to be a lousy beach day. I reach over for my beach cover-up. Tuck's always paying attention to those kinds of things. Especially on vacation. Always studying the sky, pointing at clouds, checking the wind. Of course, if you're Tuck, it's nice to know whether you're going to be buried in snow when you wake up in the morning or if the rain's going to wash away the trail or the tent's going to blow away in the wind. And if makes me very happy that those are things I don't have to worry about.

The thing I do keep worrying about is what's going to happen when we both get home. We've never gone so long without talking as we did before we left. Five whole days, and all we said to each other were things like, "Did you tell the post office to hold the mail?" I sneezed once and he didn't even bless me.

He left before me. His friends picked him up at three A.M. and I had to listen to his hiking boots going back and forth across the rug and "Hey, anybody bring any nylon tape?" and "I got a great deal on this new bag. Good to fifty below" until I thought I was going to cry.

Then there was a lot of car doors slamming and Tuck was back in the bedroom and I thought, *He couldn't do it. I knew he couldn't just leave me like this.* But he just leaned down and kissed me on the forehead. And that made me want to cry, too.

I almost said *have a good time.* Because it seemed so awful for us to go off mad for two whole weeks. But then I thought how it was all his fault in the first place, and it made me mad and sorry for myself all over again. So I just lay there and let him think I was asleep.

He left me a note. I found it when I got up. *Have fun at the beach, it said. Love, Tuck. P.S. See you on Thursday the 28th. We'll spend the long weekend together.* And that made me mad, too, because he'd thought of doing it and I hadn't.

A gust of wind whips along the beach, taking my paper cup with it and I have to get up and chase it along the sand. I stuff it into my bag. Along with my sunglasses and a box of crackers and the sun block I didn't use.

The water's not flat gray anymore. It's curly and white-topped and the blowing sand is stinging my ankles. Definitely time to give up on the beach. I shake out my blanket and the wind takes it, holds it straight out, then the wind dies and the blanket collapses. I drape it over my arm, grab my bag and start crossing the sand toward the cottage. I'll spend the afternoon finishing my book, maybe send some emails. Maybe even write to Tuck and send it by carrier pigeon. "Having an okay time," it will say. "Wish you were here."

Maybe it's the sound of the wind behind me blowing across the empty beach or the sky that's getting dark and feels like it's pressing down on me, but I really mean that last part. I really wish he were here.

***

The way I like nature is seeing it the way I'm seeing it now. Through a window. Especially the way it's acting. It must be the edge of the hurricane as it blows out to sea. But the water's crashing up the beach and so high you'd almost think it was coming right up under the cottage. And the wind, the sound of it, the way it makes the cottage shake. If this is a hurricane missing us by a hundred miles, I hate to think what happens if it's right on target.

The window rattles and I decide to make myself a cup of tea. I sit in the little kitchenette waiting for the water to boil so I can ignore what's going on outside. Then the lights flicker, go out, come back on, then go out again and stay out.

I find a flashlight and a box of candles in a cupboard, which must mean this happens all the time. I light a few candles in the kitchen and a few in the living room and think that if Tuck were here it would almost be fun. Then there's a big crash on the bedroom side of the cottage and a warm, wet wind pours through the cottage, making all the candles flicker and go out.

I move slowly toward the bedroom, playing the flashlight back and forth. There's glass all over the bed and the rug. Splintered wood and a big hole where the window used to be.

That's when I decide I'm going home.

I take as much stuff as I can fit in one bag, put on my bright pink raincoat, which I almost didn't bring, and open the front door, just enough to see what it's like. The wind almost blows me and the door smack against the wall. It takes some pushing to close it again, and then I go through the kitchenette and out the back door, where there's at least some house between me and the wind. I don't spend much time looking around, but I could swear the house is in the ocean. No sand. No beach. Just water all the way up onto the road.

I turn the car radio on and turn the volume up high. It's a roar out there now, and the announcer sounds excited. "Tides ten to fifteen feet above normal ... evacuating low-lying areas ... shelters open ... Priam's Point Road already impassable."

Priam's Point. *I'm* on Priam's Point.

I decide if I ever see Nathan again I'll kill him.

"Stay calm," I tell myself out loud. I take deep breaths and wonder what to do. And I realize that I'm not the person to ask. The person to ask is 250 miles away on top of some mountain where the sun is probably shining. What would he do? I ask myself. What would Tuck do at this very moment? I imagine him sitting there next to me. "Got to get to the safest shelter," he says.

"Safest shelter," I repeat and think hard. There are only two cottages, a shack bar, and a boathouse out here. The cottages and the snack bar are new, but the boathouse looks like it's been here for a hundred years. I close my eyes and picture Tuck. "It's been here a hundred years," he says. "Figure it out, Lizzy."

It takes me forever to get to the boathouse. When a really big wind comes, I have to drop on my hands and knees in the water and wait till it's gone so I won't get blown away. I stay near the posts that line the edge of the road, because they're the only things above water. That's something Tuck says to do: "Always keep yourself well-oriented."

The boathouse is open on both ends, and water's rushing through. Other things too — pieces of wood, barrels. I keep shining the flashlight around so I won't get hit and look for a way to get up higher. Then I see stairs, and halfway to them something whacks me in the back of the legs and keeps going by. I shine my light at it. It's a small open crate, and there's something in it. Something small, with wet fur and shiny green eyes. Its mouth is moving but the sound is lost in the noise of the wind.

I really want to get up those stairs, but I can't take my flashlight off that kitten as it floats further away. Is this the way Tuck felt when he spent half a day climbing up and down a fifty-foot tree to put a baby owl back in its nest?

When I finally get to the top of the boathouse, I close the door to the stairs and lean against it. It almost seems quiet once the door's shut. That's when I start to shake. My teeth chatter. I'm soaked. And freezing. The flashlight beam makes little jumps around the room. There's a rug on the floor, a couple of blankets on wooden chairs, two cases of beer stacked in a corner, bags of potato chips and popcorn. A good place for kids to have a party.

I take the kitten out of my raincoat pocket and set it down on the floor. Then I peel off my wet clothes and spread them on the floor. I wrap a blanket around me, eat some potato chips and sip a little warm beer.

"Stay warm, keep up your strength, don't get dehydrated," Tuck says.

"Anything else?" I ask.

"Get some rest."

I stand there, still shivering, listening to the roar outside. "Fat chance," I say, and sip more beer.

***

Picking Tuck's note out of the wastebasket again, I uncrumple it and read it. Then I wad it up and toss it back in. "See you Thursday," it says, and here it is Friday afternoon and he's still not here. Having such a good time he can't come home when he promised. And there I could have been washed out to sea and never heard from again and he would never even know about it.

I take another bite of my triple-decker peanut butter-and-fluff sandwich. The kitten watches me from the sofa cushion he's picked as his very own. I saved his life. He's my responsibility now. I walk over to the window. Everything is still a mess, even here. Trees down, no cell phone service, no electricity. The house across the street has a piece of plywood where the picture window used to be.

I watch a National Guard jeep come swerving down the street. It just misses two downed trees and a parked car. I came home in one just like it, except my driver wasn't insane. It pulls into our driveway, half runs over the yew I planted last year.

"Hey," I say, "What …"

Then Tuck jumps out from behind the wheel and races across the yard to the door. He looks like a fireman — long yellow raincoat, hip boots. His hair's a mess. The front door slams against the wall, he throws it open so hard. He stands there, staring at me. "Where have you been?" he yells.

I jump. "Where have *I* been?" I yell back. "Where have *you* been?"

"Where have *I* been? I've been looking for *you*!" He looks as bad as I must have when I finally got out of that boathouse.

"Looking for *me*?" I say.

"There was nothing there," he says, his voice going wobbly. "No cottage. Nothing. The car was empty, sitting in five feet of water." He looks at me. "Lizzy." And then he's holding me like he thought he'd never do it again.

We both start talking at the same time. He tells me how he heard about the storm veering back to land, how he ran down the mountain, drove to the beach, wrecked Max's car, stole the jeep.

I tell him how there was water everywhere and the wind was a roar, how scared I was but how it was as if he was telling me what to do every minute.

"You wrecked Max's car? You stole the jeep?"

"Don't worry," he says. "We'll get it all straightened out." Then he sees the kitten, which is scratching its ear. "What's that?"

"That's Nathan," I say.

"Nathan?"

"It's a long story."

He gives me a long kiss. "You could tell me now," he says. "Or you could tell me later."

"I think later would be nice."

It's a very good compromise.

———

STARRY NIGHT

"**You** can probably slow down a little," I say, teasing. "I mean, your folks didn't give us a deadline, did they? Be here by three or we lock the door!"

Gary's foot eases off the gas and the blur out the window turns into stone walls and green fields and patches of woods.

"Nice," I say, and turn off the AC, roll down my window, breathe in some real country summer air for a change. "Two days," I remind him. "No crucial meetings, no deadlines, no crises. Remember?"

He adjusts his gold-rimmed sunglasses, looks at me, smiles. At least his mouth smiles. I assume his eyes are smiling, too, but I can't see them behind those mirror lenses. All I can see is my own reflection. Which he knows I find very disconcerting. "It's their intention," he tells me, "to disconcert. Gives one the upper hand right off the bat."

And if anyone knows about upper hands, it's Gary. It's one of the reasons his ad business has tripled its client list in just two years. "So, there's no one else at home like you?" I ask.

His mouth smiles again. "Out here? Could you imagine anyone like me out here?"

I look back out my window at the weathered barns and the cows grazing on the sides of green hills and know there probably aren't many power lunches going on, not many high-stress ad presentations or all-night brain drains.

"I think I was ten years old when I started getting restless," he says.

I try to imagine a ten-year-old Gary. While all the other kids ran home after school to eat chocolate chip cookies and go rollerblading, he was organizing his friends into sales forces and offering them ten percent of all the magazine subscriptions they could sell. Then I try to picture his family ... his mother, his father, his little brother, and imagine them all wondering where on earth Gary had come from. Wondering if maybe there'd been a mix-up at the hospital and he really belonged to some couple jetting between New York and Los Angeles, who happened to stop in Turner's Falls just long enough to give birth.

Gary and I are at a marriage crossroads. His high-powered lifestyle is giving me doubts and Gary can't begin to understand why I'm even giving that a second thought. Our life is going to be one whirlwind of success, he tells me. How could you even think of turning that down? Then his phone rings and I groan.

"Sorry, Jess," he says. "It should only take a minute."

Right. But then I already know that business comes first. And I also know that what Gary wants, Gary gets. It's the reason I'm driving to Turner's Falls with him. And it's all happened so fast I can hardly believe it myself. But then, that's Gary for you. Whatever resistance I might have put up was nothing against his persistence.

"That was the architect," Gary says. "They're going to start the remodel on Monday."

"Monday? But we haven't even see the latest plans."

"I took care of it already," he says. "There were only a few minor changes and he needed approval to lock in the demolition work for Monday."

"Oh." I have the feeling something's gotten past me here, but half an hour before meeting his parents probably isn't the time to start dealing with it.

He looks at his watch, the newest model, which seems to do everything except brush his teeth. "Guess we'll stop and see Carl first," he says, "since we go right by the nursery anyway.

And there's no telling when he'll show up at my folks' or if he'll show up at all."

Carl is Gary's younger brother. All I really know about him is that he has a degree in plant biology. Gary had shaken his head when he told me. "Plant biology," he said, as though the two words didn't quite make sense to him. "He knows he can have a job with me any time, but he keeps fooling around with that greenhouse of his."

"Maybe that's what makes him happy," I suggested.

"Or maybe he just doesn't know which end is up," he said.

Sometimes Gary seems to think he knows what's better for you than you do yourself. Which reminds me about Monday and the call from the architect.

We drive under an arbor of maple trees, their high, green branches stretching across the road to touch each other, and I wonder if I lived here, if I'd get restless like Gary. Or if I'd spend a lot of time talking walks and painting.

"There it is," Gary says. He points up ahead to the left. "Carl's place." It has weathered board siding and lots of windows and a roof that's half glass and half solar panels. We pull up in front just as Gary's phone rings again. "You go in," he says. "I'll only be a minute."

Stepping inside the greenhouse is like stepping into a different world. The air smells intensely like earth and green grass, reminds me of the smells in my mother's garden, something I haven't thought about in a very long time. And even though I haven't grown a thing in years, I have a sudden urge to try something simple … a begonia on my kitchen windowsill.

I walk over to the rows of plants looming under the glass roof and find I remember their names … phlox, impatiens, cosmos, Shasta daisies. And a plant that's pink and red and gorgeous that I've never seen before. I feel something touch my hair and look up at pots of lush ferns hanging just above my head. I reach up and touch the fronds. "Absolutely beautiful," I say.

"I think so, too."

I turn around. It's almost like seeing Gary, but a different Gary. A Gary who didn't get restless. Who doesn't have his shirts specially made. Who wears dirty sneakers and forgets to have regular haircuts. A Gary who doesn't look like he's on his way somewhere even when he's standing still.

I'm too surprised by the resemblance to do anything but stare for a second. He folds his arms across his chest, smiles. "I talk to them, too," he says. "I think they like it."

"Carl?" I say, putting out my hand. "I'm Jessica. Gary's still in the car."

His smile fades, then comes back, just not quite as warm as it was before. "Jessica," he says, "of course." He starts to take my hand, then stops. "I've been digging out back. My hands are dirty."

"It's okay. I used to paint. I was always covered in it. Goes with the territory, no?"

His smile warms again and he takes my hand. "Gary's outside?"

"On the phone. I enjoyed the ride. It's beautiful here. How about a tour? Show me what you've been digging. But first, tell me what this is." I point to the pink and red blossoms.

"That is a cattleya orchid," he says. "I'm starting to propagate them."

"It's so beautiful. I was thinking I'd like to try my luck with something, but something easy, something that would have a better than even chance despite my black thumb."

He laughs. He isn't wearing mirror sunglasses, so I can see his eyes. And that makes me think that Gary may be wrong. It's really eye contact that gives a person the upper hand.

Carl takes me through the greenhouse. He answers every question I ask. "This is a plant you could manage with no trouble," he says. "And this." One is an ivy, the other a spider plant. He shows me a seed bed with tender green shoots just nudging through the soil. "You're a painter?"

"Painter? Oh, no." I shake my head. "I painted for a while, but it never came to anything. And I needed to pay the rent and eat once in a while. So I started doing interior decorating instead." I lean down near a flat of lily of the valley, something I haven't smelled since I was a little girl. "That's how I met your brother. I decorated his offices. And here I am."

"Well, maybe you can get back to painting eventually. Once you and Gary are married."

That's not something I've thought about. That I might not have to hustle sixty hours a week. That I might be able to carve out time for painting. But somehow that doesn't feel right. Besides, there's no studio on the architect's plans for our remodel. I shrug. "Maybe."

Carl is putting the two plants he wants me to take on the counter when Gary walks in. They slap each other on the back, seem happy to see each other, but not quite sure what to do about it.

"How's business?" Gary asks.

"Staying afloat," Carl says. "How about you?"

Gary gives him a thumb's up, then looks around. "Lots of plants," he says.

"That's the idea," Carl says.

Then a car drives up. "Customers," Gary says. "That's good."

Carl nods.

"We'll get going then," Gary says. "You coming up to the house for dinner?"

Carl looks as though he's got this one rehearsed. "Yeah," he says, slowly, almost as if he's surprised he's saying it. "Yeah. I'll be there."

Gary looks surprised, too. "Great. We'll see you later then."

Carl smiles at me. "Don't forget your plants."

"Plants?" Gary looks at me, puzzled.

I point to the counter. "Those are mine"

"In the car? There'll be dirt all over the place."

"No," I say. "They'll be fine." Gary and I stare at each other.

"No problem," Carl says. "I'll bring them with me. And I'll wrap them up. Nice and clean."

"Sorry," Gary says, when we're in the car. "I didn't get what you were up to at first."

"What I was up to?"

"Carl's plants. Buying them. Helping him out." He smiles at me behind his glasses. "We'll do the whole house in plants when it's finished. The offices, too. That should help his profit margin for the quarter."

I could tell him Carl's giving me the plants and wouldn't let me pay. That he doesn't seem hard up. But it's basically a nice thing Gary wants to do, so I don't say anything, just smile back

At dinner that night, Gary excuses himself before dessert to make "a few phone calls."

"Well that means more dessert for the rest of us," his dad says, "because he won't be back until we're all in bed," and everybody laughs. His mother brings in a fudge cake and cuts everyone a piece. "I'll put Gary's piece in the fridge," she tells me. When she begins to clear the table I get up to help, but she makes it clear that she'd just as soon do it herself. "No arguments," she says. "I'm the only one who knows how to load the dishwasher. And you two," she looks at me and Carl, should go out and take a walk. It's a lovely bright night, and Jess can see a little of where Gary grew up." Her voice is soft, but no one argues. Gary's dad gives me a wink and at least now I know where Gary got his take-charge personality.

Outside, it's a warm, moonlit night, and the sky is full of more stars than I've seen in a long time. Carl points. "Ursa Major," he says, "the Big Dipper. See it?"

I nod.

"And Draco," he says. "See that line of stars between the bowls of the Big Dipper and the Little Dipper? How it twists down and around? That's Draco, the dragon."

"I used to know some of them," I tell him, "but I don't think I've looked up at night for a while."

"Too many city lights to see much of anything," he says. And then we both point at a shooting star. "Did you see it?" we ask at the same time. We walk down one long road then turn onto another. We take turns talking, and after a while, I realize we've walked a lot farther than we intended.

"We should head back," I say, "it must be late." We both stop and turn toward one another. I can see him clearly in the moonlight, and when I look at him, I don't see Gary anymore, I see Carl. I see the easy way he stands and the way he locks me with his eyes. The way his hair curls against the collar of his white cotton shirt and the way his forearms are hard and muscled from digging and lifting. I feel something I shouldn't be feeling and I try to put it out of my mind, because it must just be the soft air and the moon and Carl's resemblance to Gary making me feel this way.

Then Carl puts his hand out as though he's going to touch my face, but he stops, lets his hand fall. We don't say a word all the way back.

When we finally walk up the porch steps, Gary is sitting there waiting. "I was going to give you two about five more minutes before I called out the National Guard."

I laugh. "We went a little farther than we intended."

"Mom's planning a cookout tomorrow," Gary says. He looks at Carl. "You can come, can't you?"

Carl nods. "Sure." He backs toward his car in the driveway. "See you both tomorrow."

But the next day, he doesn't come to the cookout.

"He's like that," Gary says, "disorganized. He probably started fooling around at the greenhouse and lost track of time." He hands me a paper plate with a hamburger on it. I lift the bun and see he's already put ketchup and mustard on it. Trouble is, that's the way *he* likes his burger. I hate ketchup, and you'd think he'd know that by now. But I say nothing. Just eat the hamburger, ketchup and all, and along with his mom and dad, listen to his story about his latest advertising campaign.

***

For a whole month, I keep waiting for it to go away, that feeling that's been sitting in my stomach ever since my walk with Carl. But it won't go. And it makes me do funny things. When Gary takes me over to the house to see what the remodeling crew has done so far, I walk into what used to be a big roomy kitchen and can't figure out what I'm looking at. "Where did these walls come from?" I ask Gary.

"It's what we decided on," Gary says. "To cut the kitchen in half and use the extra space for a work-out room."

"*We* decided that?"

"Well, I guess *I* did. And the architect. It made much more sense than wasting all that room on a kitchen."

"To *you* maybe. And, I guess, to the architect. But not to me. Tell them to put the walls back where they were."

Gary looks at me. He doesn't seem to know what to say.

And then that night we go to a new restaurant. "Two blackened swordfish," he tells the waiter. He smiles at me. "I've heard it's the best thing on the menu," he tells me.

"It must be if you're having two." I look up at the waiter. "I'll have the eggplant parmesan."

Gary chokes on his water.

***

So now I'm sitting and staring out the window at the buildings across the street, trying to wish away this feeling that keeps rocking the boat, trying to reason with myself that if I ignore it long enough, it will surely go away and things will go back to normal. Then the phone rings and it's Gary telling me

21

he has to catch the next shuttle to New York, because a very big opportunity has come up and he'll be gone the whole weekend. It may be my imagination, but he almost sounds relieved. I hang up and look out at the little bit of city sky I can see, and the longer I sit there, the bigger the feeling gets until I can't ignore it anymore.

By the time I get to Turner's Falls, the sky is going red on the horizon, and as I drive under the canopy of maple branches, it almost feels like coming home.

Carl's leaning against the greenhouse doorway, watching as I get out of the car, looking more than a little surprised.

"You forgot to give me my plants," I tell him. "The ones you said even my black thumb couldn't kill. You were supposed to bring them to the cookout. The one you missed."

For a second, he doesn't say anything, just looks at me, then he shrugs. "It occurred to me that maybe they'd just complicate your life," he says. "That maybe things would stay simpler without them."

"Don't tell me you do it, too," I say. "Tell people what's best for them instead of letting them figure that out for themselves."

He shakes his head. "Not me. It's just that the way we both seemed to be feeling that night ... if we let it happen again ... I mean, it might make things a little awkward. At the next family gathering, for instance?"

"Not any more awkward than a bad match. And I think that fact has dawned on more than just you and me lately."

He holds his hand out. I can see he's been working in the dirt. That he still hasn't gotten a haircut. That his shirt has a tear in it and his jeans are muddy. And I decide that the first painting I'm going to try will be of him. Looking just this way.

———

LIFE'S LITTLE SURPRISES

Hannah moved around the kitchen, not letting herself look at the calendar. Not even once. Because those thick black numbers in their neat, self-righteous squares had been growing bigger and bigger, almost jumping off the wall. Any day now they were going to start announcing themselves out loud.

Today's the thirteenth, " *Hannah, have you told him yet?*

Today's the fourteenth, Hannah. You've known for almost eight weeks now. Have you told him yet?

As if it weren't the only thing she'd been thinking about. Eight weeks. Fifty-six days. And practically every hour of every day she made up her mind to tell him. But then she didn't. And the longer she waited, the more impossible it became.

So now it was eight weeks since she'd first suspected, and Chris still didn't know he was going to be a father.

She took six eggs out of the refrigerator, then went back after the butter, the milk, the spinach. Tonight was the night. It definitely had to be tonight.

She looked at the cookbook propped against the flour canister. On a stress scale of one to ten, spinach soufflé rated a twelve. Maybe it was all that breaking, separating, heating, whipping. She lifted a soufflé dish down from the cupboard, slipped the whisk off the wall hook and wondered why things couldn't just go along the way they were supposed to. Smoothly, without a hitch.

She sighed, set the bowl and whisk on the counter and looked at the wall chart over the table. It was all there. Their whole life at a glance. At least the first five years. Because Chris believed in visualization ... that it was important to *see* things, not just *think* about them. So he'd worked on it one whole weekend, using colored markers, making funny little drawings — a house with a picket fence and smoke coming out the chimney. "I'm figuring on year four for the house," he'd told her. "As long as the rate of inflation holds steady. And since your car should be good for at least another fifty-thousand miles, we'll put that expenditure into year five."

It was the kind of thing you got used to, being married to an investment counselor. He like to manage things. Everything. Time, money, the future. And he hated surprises.

She scanned the timeline — house; new cars; cross-country trip; job promotions for them both; an Oriental rug because it was a good investment, beautiful, and useful all at the same time. Everything was there in a nice, logical, well-planned progression. Everything except a baby.

And now Chris was going to come home, walk into the kitchen, and right away know something was up. Before she even said a word. Because almost three years of marriage had taught him that spinach soufflé meant trouble. Along with three-layer cakes, chocolate mousse, and veal steaks.

"Do you have any idea what you're doing to my digestion?" he'd told her after they were married. It's not fair. You've turned all my expectations upside down. My salivary glands don't know what to do anymore. I mean, jeez, Hannah, since when does making a guy a triple-layer chocolate cake with chocolate icing mean he's in trouble? Whenever I walk into the kitchen and smell something great, I figure the car got totaled or my boss called and said I'm fired."

He was right. And it wasn't fair. But she just couldn't help it. Reaching for a cookbook when she was stressed out was automatic. Like saying *bless you* when somebody sneezed. And she'd tried not cooking. Like when Betty Mumford in the next apartment had called and asked if Chris would open her windows because they'd been painted last fall and here it was just absolutely the most beautiful spring evening, wasn't it, and her silly old windows wouldn't open, and Chris was so big and strong, and Hannah wouldn't mind if she borrowed him for just a few ll'l old minutes, now would she??

Hannah hadn't minded. At least not for the first five or ten li'l old minutes. Because Betsy Mumford wasn't Chris's type. Even if she was attractive and a size six and had a voice that dripped Tennessee charm. But then it got to be fifteen minutes and twenty and more than a half-hour — and how long did it take to open three or four stuck windows?

After fifty minutes, she'd started thinking about chicken croquettes with sour-milk gravy, zucchini in dill sauce, and lemon meringue pie. But if she started cooking, then he'd know something was bothering her. So she'd resisted. She'd cleaned out the linen closet instead, which didn't do a thing for her. She'd scrubbed the tub, which didn't help a bit. Finally, she'd put her ear against the wall separating the two apartments, which didn't do any good either because she couldn't hear a thing ... whatever *that* meant.

And when he did finally come home one hour and eleven minutes later, she was sitting on her hands, trying hard not to think about homemade breadcrumbs and new potatoes.

"Hi," he'd said, closing the door behind him.

Silence.

"Uh — the windows were pretty stuck ... and then she asked if I'd change a bulb, and she needed help moving the sofa ... and then she insisted on making me a drink, and it would have been rude to say no, since she was already fixing it."

The silence had lasted twenty-eight hours. Until she got up in the middle of the next night and started making super-chocolate chunk, walnut, coconut cookies. Her silence had cracked along with the eggs. "You go over there for ten minutes," she muttered while she creamed the butter and sugar," and end up staying an extra hour!"

Chris had come into the kitchen just as the first batch was done.

"It's three a.m.," he'd said.

"Oh," she'd said, "so you can tell time after all."

"Hey, you talked," he said.

She'd held a cookie out to him. "The next time Betsy Mumford asks you to unstick her windows or change her bulb or move her sofa," Hannah said, "we'll tell her you're just about to catch a plane for South America. Agreed?"

"Agreed," he said, kissing her on the lips before he popped the cookie in his mouth.

After that, she went with her urges. When she felt like cooking, she didn't fight it. If things went wrong, she cooked and then things got better. But this time, what was she going to do? Cook her way through the next seven months?

Chris came home while she was pricking the popovers. At first he didn't say a word. Then, "You lost that new account?"

"I did not lose the account. It's going very well, actually."

"Your car broke down on the way to work?"

"My car's fine."

"It's Betsy Mumford," he said, frowning, looking at the spinach soufflé, taking off his coat. "Is that it? She called again. She wants me to come over and move her refrigerator, unplug her sink ... something like that?"

Hannah pushed hard against the cold-water faucet handle, which did no good because the water kept dripping anyway. She handed him the popovers, picked up the soufflé, carried it into the dining room and sat down.

"It's not Betsy Mumford," she said. "It's not my job, not my car, your mother didn't call. It's none of those things."

He stared hard at her and his eyes started going from amber to chocolate, the way they did when he got intense. It was one of the first things she'd noticed about him. The way his eyes changed color with his moods. Along with the fact that he was so interested in everything she had to say, and how he'd wanted to know everything about her right away ... where she was going, where she'd been and what she'd been doing there, what she was going to do when she got to Los Angeles. And it was always strange to think that if the train hadn't been so crowded, they might not have met at all. Although he always said he would have sat down next to her even if every other seat had been empty.

"Because as soon as I saw you," he said, "I knew I had to talk to you. And as soon as I talked to you, I knew I was in love."

"Even though you didn't plan it that way?"

"Even though I didn't plan it that way."

"You mean you're just traveling around with no plans?" he'd asked her on the bus. "No idea of what you're going to do from one day to the next?"

"All I know," she'd told him, "is that I have a ticket for Los Angeles. And right now, that's good enough for me."

He was going only as far as Denver.

Except in Denver, he'd gotten off the train and bought a ticket to Salt Lake City because that was as far out of his way as he could make himself go at that moment, and in Salt Lake City, he'd gotten off and bought a ticket to Reno, and in Reno he'd bought a ticket to L.A.

"What about your plans?" she'd asked him.

"What plans?" he'd said.

It was the only spontaneous thing he'd ever done. But at least he'd picked the right time to do it. And if he could do it once, couldn't he do it again?

He leaned toward her across the table and her practiced speech evaporated. She was going to blurt it out with no preparation and he was going to go into shock because his entire five-year plan would have to be scratched. She took a deep breath. "We're pregnant."

He blinked.

For a moment, the only noise was the faucet dripping in the sink, which grew louder and louder in the silence.

Then Chris sat back. He smiled. "Funny, Hannah. Very funny. Now tell me what's *really* wrong."

She stared at him. Was it so bad he simply couldn't believe it? Something that wasn't on his time line and, therefore, couldn't possibly happen to them?

She stood up fast, bumping the table, and the soufflé wobbled and started to go flat. She went back into the kitchen, opened a drawer and took out a colored marker. She heard him come up behind her just as she was finishing the last wheel on the baby carriage. She'd drawn it right in the middle of their cross-country trip, probably when they'd have been driving through the Tetons in Idaho or Wyoming.

"There," she said, handing him the marker. "Does that help?" Then she went upstairs and slammed the bedroom door.

It wasn't as if she'd expected him to go all silly ... pick her up and carry her over to the couch, put a pillow behind her back, get her a glass of milk and a dish of pickles, maybe massage her feet. But she'd at least expected him to *believe* her.

The door opened. "Hannah?" He walked over, sat down on the bed next to her. "Guess you weren't kidding." Then he didn't say anything, just took one of her hands in both of his. "The thing about a surprise," he said, after a while, "is it's only a surprise for an instant. You know, those first few seconds when you're caught totally off-guard and you just stand there with your mouth open or you say something incredibly dumb." He squeezed her hand. "Like I did downstairs just now."

He lifted her hand, put her fingers against his lips, then against his cheek. "You know me, Hannah. I like to know what's coming. And this ... I had no idea ... I think it's great. In fact, I think it's the best news I've ever heard in my life."

She looked at him. "You do?"

He nodded. His eyes were darker than she'd ever seen them. "You weren't kidding downstairs a few minutes ago and I'm not kidding now."

"It's not in our plans," she said, looking into his eyes.

"It is now."

"Babies are notorious for turning your life upside down."

"We'll learn to walk on the ceiling."

"You won't get a good night's sleep for months."

"I'll take naps."

"We'll lose my income for a while, maybe even more than a while."

"That's why we have a savings account."

"We're going to have to cancel our cross-country trip. And you've been planning that trip for years."

"We'll just postpone it," he said, "till Junior's big enough to wear his own backpack." He smiled. "Or *her* own backpack."

She leaned against him.

"A father," he said, after a while. "I'm going to be a father."

"It's okay," she said, "you'll have seven months to plan it all out."

"C'mon," he said, "let's go down and have dinner."

"Dinner? Cold, caved-in soufflé and deflated popovers?"

He smiled. "We'll pretend you planned it that way."

***

When she woke up the next morning, Chris wasn't in bed. She put on her bathrobe, brushed her teeth, and got down to the kitchen just as he was taping a new timeline onto the wall. "Couldn't sleep," he said. He looked at the new timeline. "What do you think?"

She narrowed her eyes and studied it.

"See," he said, "if we forget the vacations, one of the new cars, and the ski lessons, and postpone the cross-country trip for a while, we can move the house up to right now — we're going to need the extra room, right? And here..." he pointed at a list of things taped up beside the timeline, "...you better go over this and add to it. It's things we'll need — you know, stroller, crib, diapers ... it's all I could think of so I know I missed stuff."

She plugged in the coffee maker, shook her head. "I don't think you've missed much." She felt light enough to float. All that worrying for nothing. She looked at the remains of last night's soufflé still sitting near the sink. No more soufflés, no more exotic desserts. The most complicated thing she'd whip up would be a bowl of popcorn. She took the soufflé and scraped it into the disposal.

"We'll have to check out schools," Chris said. "And colleges."

"Maybe we could wait a while for that," she said, reaching for the cornflakes. "Until he can roll over by himself?"

***

Several weeks later, she was staring at the sonogram image. The new one she'd taped next to the earlier two on the refrigerator. She'd been staring at it or thinking about it almost every minute since she'd come home from her appointment yesterday. And if Chris hadn't had a late meeting last evening, he probably would have been staring at it, too.

She stopped staring at the sonogram and stared at Chris's new timeline. Then she took the frozen waffles out of the toaster and threw them in the sink.

She opened the refrigerator and took out eggs, milk, lemon, bacon. And when Chris came down to breakfast, she was stirring the hollandaise sauce and the smell of sizzling Canadian bacon was everywhere.

He came up behind her, kissed her on the back of the neck. Then he stopped, looked at the pans on the stove. He peered through the oven door at the biscuits. He cleared his throat. "Hannah, is there any chance this is a celebration breakfast?

"Celebration?" She kept stirring the sauce.

"All this," he said, sounding a little hesitant. "Eggs Benedict, biscuits." He came up beside her, put his face right next to hers so it was hard to avoid looking at him. "Hannah, talk to me."

"It's visualization," she said. "That's a very important concept according to you, right?"

She lifted the foil off the two dishes, each with two pieces of bacon and two eggs. Then she took the saucepan off the stove and began spooning hollandaise over the eggs. "Sometimes," she said, "it's easier to visualize something than it is to talk about it."

She handed him one of the plates. "Like this," she said. She opened the oven, lifted out two biscuits and put one on either side of his plate. Then she went over and sat down at the table.

He looked at her. "Visualize?" He sat down opposite her. "I haven't a clue what you mean."

"Look at your plate, Chris. What do see exactly?"

He looked at his plate. "Two pieces of Canadian bacon," he said. "Two poached eggs. Hollandaise sauce. And two biscuits."

She nodded. "Aside from the sauce, what does everything have in common?"

He looked at her. "Two of everything?"

She looked back at him. At the person who'd decided not to get off the train in Denver. "Two of everything," he said again. And then very softly, "of *everything*?"

She nodded. She could see him wrestling with it. Because he really didn't like surprises, and more unexpected things had happened to him in the last few weeks than had probably happened in his whole life. Except for her. Except for the train and falling in love.

And then he did something that made all the tension go away. Made her see that she'd gone to all the trouble of eggs Benedict and biscuits for nothing. Made her see that he really did know there were things more important than timelines and goals and plans and management. He simply leaned across the kitchen table and kissed her — twice.

BEWITCHED

Sarah buckled her seat belt, put the car into drive, checked her rear-view mirror, and backed right into the fence.

Damn. How had *that* happened?

She looked down at the shift knob. In reverse. Not drive. She got out, checked the fence, the bumper. Both okay. But she could have sworn she'd pushed the shift knob forward, not backward.

She pulled on her right ear lobe. Something was wrong.

She got back into the car, disconnected it from the fence, sat there for a second thinking.

Too many strange things were happening. Like all the leaves falling off her plants. Practically overnight. Hundreds of perfectly healthy green leaves lying there on the floor. And her stereo. She hadn't been able to listen to any of her James Taylor CDs. All they did was whisper. She didn't get it. And what about not being able to get anything to stick? The stamps falling off envelopes, the envelope flaps refusing to stay closed. And her phone changing its ring tone. *She* hadn't programmed it to do that. In fact, it was playing a tune that wasn't even *on* her phone. A strange tune. Something familiar she couldn't quite place.

And then last week when she was leaving the office for that ten o'clock meeting and Maureen stopped her at the door. "New fad?" Maureen said, looking down at Sarah's shoes. "You know, my three-year-old has that same problem." She still couldn't believe that one. A black shoe and a white shoe. Now how did a thing like *that* happen? She was dead certain she'd put on her gray heels.

She turned the rear-view mirror down a bit so she could see herself. Was she coming down with something? Viruses had weird effects sometimes. But she looked okay. Normal. No flush. One gray eye and one green eye looked back at her. She looked fine, just fine.

She turned the mirror back to its normal position, sighed. Maybe she needed an energy tap, a little meditation might help. Just to make sure everything was in alignment.

She shut off the engine, made sure her seat belt was snug. No more energy taps in the car without her belt on. Not since the time she found herself several inches off the seat, her head rising through the open sun roof, two old women staring at her from the sidewalk. Not that those kinds of things happened very often. But once in a while, when the astral energy was just right.

She closed her eyes, took a deep breath, became an empty vessel filling, filling, filling with calming lavender light.

But then she suddenly became something that was emptying, emptying, emptying. She opened her eyes. Wonderful. She'd developed a leak. Wasn't anything ever going to work properly again?

And just when she was supposed to be closing the Boyer account. Great.

She pulled on her ear. It was Boyer. It had to be. That's when her problems started. Her chemistry had been all out of whack ever since she'd first walked into his office. But why? Yes, Jefferson Boyer was a tough nut to crack. But tough nuts were her specialty. Isn't that why Emil had given her the account in the first place?

"This could be the biggest account we've ever snagged," Emil told her. "That's why I'm sending *you*." And then he'd looked at her in that sort of musing way he had. "How do you do it, Sarah?" She'd shrugged. Tried to look as though it were as much of a mystery to her. "Cast some kind of spell, huh?" he'd said. That made her smile.

"Well," he'd said, "it better be a pretty good one this time, because Preston's after Boyer, too. And I hear he's got a new man — Carson or Carlyle or something — who's supposed to be hot."

But that was four months ago, and Boyer was still seesawing like a black cat trying to make up its mind whose path to cross. It was a record for her. No account had ever taken this long before. Ever. She was actually beginning to doubt her own abilities. All her sales were down. Emil's ulcer was acting up. And there seemed to be no reason for it. No reason why everything was suddenly not going right.

She drummed her fingers on the steering wheel. Preston's new man. Red hot, huh? The connection kept clicking in her mind. Hadn't he and her problems shown up at just about the same time? She concentrated on him, wondering if, even though it had never happened before, she'd finally met her match. Maybe even someone who could best her. But that didn't make any sense, did it? Because she'd seen him. Looked straight at him. Coming into Boyer's office as she was leaving. He'd held the door for her, smiled at her as if he knew her. Which he probably did, since knowing the competition was always part of being successful.

Seeing something unusual about him would have explained a lot. Boyer's frustrating resistance to her. The fact that she wasn't functioning on all eight cylinders. Her plants, her phone. But when they met in the doorway to Boyer's office, Carson or Carlyle or whatever looked at her with two brown eyes. Two perfectly matching brown eyes.

So now what?

Her stomach growled as if it were trying to tell her something. She was going to be sitting in Jefferson Boyer's office in a little over an hour. And she was going to be sitting there like some half-deflated balloon, all floppy and out of control. Her stomach growled again. This time she listened. She started the car and pulled out of the parking lot. Doughnuts. A quick fix, but if she timed it right, maybe enough to get her through the meeting.

She stood at the counter searching the doughnut case for the right choice, waiting for one of the two counter girls to notice her. They were down at the other end, leaning their elbows on the Formica counter, giggling, forehead to forehead with two boys wearing T-shirts that said Drunken State and Budweiser U.

She cleared her throat, glanced at her watch. She hated to break up the fun, but she did have an appointment. And she did need those doughnuts.

She looked at the girls. One was a brunette. Tall. Doing a lot of smiling but not much talking. The other was taking most of the attention. Short, blond, cute, peppy.

She concentrated on the brunette, fixed the girl's arm in her mind and tugged. Nothing happened at first, but then the girl started moving toward Sarah. Sideways. As though she didn't know she was doing it. She came like molasses, but she came.

"Two honey-dipped," Sarah said, "and one sugar-raised."

***

She finished the last doughnut as she turned into Boyer's block. The energy had spread through her like honey, amber-smooth, making her feel light, almost buoyant. She felt great. Poor Carson or Carlyle. Would he be terrifically crushed when he heard she'd taken the account? He probably wasn't used to losing. Especially considering how well he'd held her off until now. She pictured his face in her mind. Nice face. Nice smile. It might have been interesting to find that he wasn't your normal, everyday, average, run-of-the-mill human being.

She looked along the sides of the street. Packed. There wasn't a parking space anywhere within four blocks. In five minutes she had to be in Boyer's office, which meant parking several blocks away was no option. She fixed her attention on the area directly in front of the Boyer building, hummed softly, made one more circle around the block. Four cars pulled away from the curb on her next pass, and three cars followed her into the empty spaces, riding the coattails of all those magic doughnuts.

***

Emil was waiting for her inside the revolving doors. "How did you do that?" he said. "I drove up and down that street for twenty minutes. And then I ended up parking ten blocks away." He looked at her as if she'd just parted the seas.

"I just got lucky," she said, setting her briefcase down on a chair. She folded her arms, looked at him. "Funny, but I don't remember Jefferson Boyer asking me to bring my boss along today."

Emil stuck his hand in his jacket pocket, pulled out a package of Tums, and popped two in his mouth. "It was either this or sit in my office and commune with my ulcer," he said. He shrugged. "Anyhow, I figured it might be helpful if the president of the company showed up. You know, to give Boyer an inkling of how very, very much we want his account. Besides, I figured at this point anything's worth a try."

"Well..." She picked up her briefcase and started toward the elevator, "you needn't have bothered. Because today I have things under perfect control." She pressed the up arrow. "Today is the day Jefferson Boyer puts his signature on our bottom line."

"You seem pretty confident," Emil said.

"I am," she said.

Then the elevator doors slid open and Carson or Carlyle was standing there with three other people, and she felt her stomach swoop, the way it did on a roller coaster.

What was *he* doing here? And why did he have such a satisfied look on that handsome face? Was she too late? Had he stolen the account while she was standing at the doughnut counter?

He was the last one out of the elevator, and he stood just outside, holding the doors from closing until she and Emil were on. His jacket brushed her hand as they passed each other. He held the doors longer than he needed to, until she finally looked up at him. Then he smiled and took his hand off the door. It slid shut, and Emil pressed fourteen. She rubbed at the prickly feeling his jacket had left on her skin.

"Glad I don't have to worry about this one anymore," Emil whispered as Boyer's secretary led them into the office. "Since you're so sure of victory, I mean."

She ignored him. Jefferson Boyer swung his big leather chair around and stood up. He looked as confused as ever. Which probably meant that Carson or Carlyle or whatever hadn't scored.

"Mr. Boyer." She took his outstretched hand. "I'd like you to meet the president of my firm…."

Jefferson Boyer looked at her, waiting.

"This is…" she said.

"Emil Spencer," Emil blurted out. He stepped forward, grabbed Boyer's hand and pumped it.

The air in the office began to change colors. Gold to bright orange to purple to green. She got dizzy.

"Let's sit down," she said, dropping into the nearest chair.

"Good idea. Let's." Jefferson Boyer sat down, too.

She wished Emil would stop staring at her. She pressed the fingertips of one hand against the other. She was leaking again. Her carbohydrate high was disappearing, flying off into that horrible green air.

"We like to think we have the best idea-people in the business," Emil was saying. "We're out to get results."

"That's what I'm interested in," Boyer said.

They all smiled at each other. It was now or never. She focused what energy she had left. *What you're interested in*, she thought at him, *is giving your account to Spencer Associates.*

"I'm also interested in giving my account to Spencer Associates," Boyer said.

And you're feeling it's time to give us a clear commitment.

"And I think it's about time I gave you a clear commitment," Boyer said.

She reached down, opened her briefcase, took out a copy of the contract and slid it across Boyer's shiny desk.

"However..." Boyer looked at the contract. Sarah blinked. His aura was doing funny things. Shifting, breaking up, coming back together. "However," he said again, "as far as signing this..." He looked up at her. "I don't think I can."

She stared at him. *You can*, she thought.

"I can't," he said.

You can, you can, you can," she insisted.

"I can't, I can't, I can't," he said.

Emil jumped up. "We understand, Jefferson. No need to get excited. We'll give you plenty of time to think it over. All the time you need." He grabbed Sarah by the elbow.

"Did you see that?" he said when they were out in the hallway. "The guy's headed for a nervous breakdown."

He pushed the down arrow at the elevator, reached in his pocket for his Tums. "And I'm not so sure about you, either. What happened to you in there?"

She shook her head. She wished she knew.

Emil chewed, the elevator doors opened, they rode down in silence.

Outside on the sidewalk, he made a face, rubbed his stomach. "Got to get a glass of milk," he said.

"I'll give you a ride," she said, "so you won't have to walk those ten blocks back to your car."

He shook his head. "Need the exercise. And you need a rest. So take tomorrow off. Forget about Boyer. Forget about his account. Just relax, okay?"

She nodded, waved as he started down the sidewalk. Poor Emil. What she should work on was giving him a nice, smooth stomach lining That is if she ever managed to do anything at all ever again.

She turned toward her car. Carson or Carlyle was leaning against the hood. She walked slowly toward him.

He smiled. "Hi," he said.

She half-smiled back.

"Can we talk?"

She thought about it. Could it make things any worse? She nodded. "Okay."

"Good," he said. He smiled. "But first I want to show you something."

She followed him along the sidewalk. He walked up behind a gray sports car.

"Mine," he said.

"Nice," she said.

He stepped out into the street, walked up to the front of the car.

"See that?"

She looked at the round yellow plastic disk attached to his front wheel. "A boot," she said. "Don't you ever pay your tickets?"

"Never got a ticket in my life," he said. He crooked his finger, started back down the street.

She followed. Slowly. What now, she wondered.

He stopped next to her car, crossed his arms, looked at her. She stared at the boot on her front wheel. She couldn't believe it. It had to be some stupid mistake.

"It's some stupid mistake," she said. "I've never had a parking ticket in my life either!"

"Look," he said, "I think we need to sit down together." He motioned toward a café across the street. "Buy you a cup of coffee?"

She hesitated. What was talking to him going to do about that thing on her car? She looked at the boot. Well, she wouldn't be going anywhere any time soon, anyway. She sighed. "Okay."

***

"Carson Carlyle." He extended his hand across the table. Out the window, their boots were visible through breaks in the traffic, along with one or two more up and down the street.

She took his hand firmly.

"You're Sarah Kennedy," he said. "My boss already warned me about you. "'Watch out for her,' he said. 'She's your competition. Walks off with all the big ones.' "

She had to smile.

"I have to tell you though, that I wasn't so worried. Competition's not something I've ever had to worry about before." He leaned back, crossed his arms. "And then all these crazy things started happening."

She sipped her coffee. "Crazy things?"

He nodded. "Take my electricity. It keeps going out. Two, three, sometimes four times a night. Electric company's been out. Electrician checked the wiring. And there's nothing wrong."

"Strange," she said.

"I'm not finished. I can't get my pens to write. Nothing but pencils now for the past two months. And tires."

"Tires?" She frowned at him.

"Six flats this week alone."

"Six?"

"Six."

"Sounds like pretty bad luck."

"That's what I thought at first," he said. "Until I got a good look at you today. At the color of your eyes."

She stared at him. He knew. But how? Then it hit her. But that couldn't be. She was looking at his eyes and they were both a very nice shade of brown.

He seemed to read her thoughts. "Haven't you ever heard of color contacts?" He looked out the window. "The boot made me mad, and I was starting to think up some heavy retaliation."

"Starting?" she said. "*Starting*? What about my plants and my stereo and my phone and my shoes and the fence and the energy leak I've developed? What about forgetting my boss's name? Are you going to tell me that wasn't *you*?"

"What about my tires and the pens and my lights? I suppose that wasn't *you*?"

"And what about the boot on my car?" They both said that at the same time.

"I have a theory," he said. "When I was about ten, I went away to camp. It was the only time I ever met someone like myself. If you know what I mean."

She nodded.

"We were in different cabins, and all the cabins competed for prizes ... neatest cabin, best divers, fastest rowers. Our two cabins never won a thing, but before the summer was half over we practically put the camp out of business."

She smiled.

"I'm serious," he said. "They had to send all of us home two weeks early. People saw shark fins in the lake. During Native American week, a counselor quit because he claimed a wooden totem chased him through the woods. The milk kept going sour, it rained for three weeks straight, and the boat house fell into the lake. And then the frogs came."

"Frogs?" She was laughing out loud now.

"They were everywhere." He waited until she was serious again. "Are you seeing a connection here?"

"I don't know," she said. "I guess it's as good an explanation as any. But we can't be sure."

"We can try an experiment," he said.

She thought about it. "Okay. But it has to be a small one."

He picked up his coffee cup. "Are you up to making some ice coffee?"

She gave him a look. "Too easy."

"Last one with a cup of hot coffee pays the bill," he said.

She concentrated, thought ice. But instead of the coffee going icy, the plant hanging above the table started to sway and leaves floated down onto the table.

"Oh boy," she said.

Then the electricity went out.

"Trust me," he said. "While we're competing against each other, neither of us is going to have any luck at all."

***

The next day, Emil called her at home. "Boyer signed," he said. "With a company I never even heard of."

She didn't know what to say. All she could think of was Carson Carlyle's second experiment.

"No more experiments," she'd told him. "Who knows what could happen."

"This time we work together," he said. "We'll try your car first. The boot on your car. Let's get rid of it."

"Oh no," she said, "not my car."

"Okay, mine."

She'd barely given it any juice, but it was like plugging into 5000 kilowatts. Up and down the street, one after the other, puffs of yellow smoke drifted into the air.

"Just like I thought," he said. And then he offered to leave. It was her territory, after all.

She considered what would happen. Her plants would grow leaves. Her phone would behave. Her shoes would match. Her sales would go up. No more competition. And no more heart-stopping meetings getting on and off the elevator.

"Let's not be hasty," she'd said.

***

She opened the refrigerator and cupboards, gathering everything that seemed right. Stock, vegetables, tiny curls of pasta, seasonings, special herbs. She hummed a little while she put together a salad, made muffins, boiled rice for a sweet pudding.

At six o'clock, she changed her clothes, put on the porch light. At six-thirty, the doorbell rang and he was standing there with her briefcase in his hand. He held it up.

"Looks like we need to make a swap."

"My briefcase? But how..." She looked at the hall table. His black briefcase was lying there. His, not hers.

"Must have happened when the lights went out," he said.

"Odd, considering it wasn't all that dark."

He shrugged, smiled.

For the first time in her life, she felt uncertain. Vulnerable. How much of his being there was her doing? How much was his? And did inviting him in mean she might never again be sure?

"There are some things that can't be controlled. Big things." He leaned toward her and she could see his eyes, eyes like her own, mismatched and maybe a little uncertain, too.

"Like falling in love," he said. "Which has a way of taking care of itself."

She felt that tingle again, opened the door wide. "You're just in time for dinner." She put out her hand, he took it, stepped inside. And just like that, the stereo clicked on and James Taylor started singing ... *how sweet it is to be loved by you...*

—

FIREWORKS

"**Katy**!" Angela yells. "Get in here. And hurry up!!"

I slide the pan of stuffed mushrooms into the oven and head for the dining room. "Now what's wrong?" But Angela isn't in the dining room. I look around. All the china, silver, table linens, and glassware are out on the buffet table, as well as silver trays of cheese and crackers. Not to mention the crystal punch bowl. All I can say is thank god Angela has a friend who works for Rent-A-Party.

"KATY!"

"I'm coming. I'm coming." I check my watch. Exactly an hour-and-a-half from now, I'll be showered and dressed, my hair will be done, and everything in the kitchen will be ready. I smile. I've done it, even though this last-minute party's been giving me nightmares ever since Steven announced we were having it.

"It's major," he told me. "My boss will be in town, and *his* boss, and *his* boss's boss. Plus some important clients. So see if you can make it special, okay?"

I wanted to ask him how he'd decided that *I* was supposed to be responsible for that — for making it 'special.' But Steven and I are at a tenuous point in our relationship and we're trying to be supportive of one another. At least that's what our pre-marital counselor says. Frankly, I seem to a be the one doing all the supporting, but I'm hoping we'll work that out.

I find Angela in the bathroom, throwing every towel in the linen closet on the floor. "What are you *doing*?" I say. Then I realize I'm standing in an inch or more of water.

"I swear," she says, "all I did was rub the pipe a little, just to get the dust off, and the whole thing split in half!" She points under the bathroom sink.

I stand there staring, too, refusing to believe this is happening.

"Call somebody, Katy," she says. "Get a plumber quick!"

The first five 24-hour plumbers don't answer at all. It takes four more calls before I finally find someone who says he'll come. "The whole bathroom is flooded," I tell him.

"I'll be there as fast as I can," he says. "Try to close any shut-off valves in the bathroom. And if that doesn't work, go down in the basement and turn those off, too."

As fast as he can is almost twenty minutes, and by then, the hall rug has become a lake.

"I turned everything I could find in the bathroom," I tell him, "but the water didn't stop." And I couldn't find anything in the basement."

"Come with me." he says, "I'll show you where it is so that if it happens again, you'll know what to do."

Very take-charge for a plumber, I think. And when we walk by Angela, her eyes get big. "*That's* a plumber?" she mouths to me.

I follow him into the cellar and he walks over to a blue valve, turns it, and upstairs, Angela lets out a whoop. He smiles at me. A very nice smile. And suddenly I'm thinking of the ski instructor I had such a crush on when I was sixteen. Same blue eyes. But why on earth am I thinking of that?

"Thank you for coming," I say. "No one else I called wanted to come out on a Saturday night. I hope this hasn't ruined your plans."

"Actually," he says, "this may be the best thing that's happened to me all day." Then he points to my bike leaning against the wall. "Nice bike," he says. "I have one, too. A slightly different model. Is it yours?"

"Yes." I go over and rub one finger across the dust on the seat. "I used to ride several times a week."

"Not anymore?"

I shake my head. "The people I do things with now don't ride. That's why it's sitting here collecting dust. I suppose I should sell it."

"Why?" he says. "Why would you sell it? Why not just get some friends who do what you like to do."

That's something Angela might say to me. Or my mother. But I don't even know this man's name. And as if he's reading my thoughts, he puts his hand out. "Mark," he says. And then Angela yells from upstairs, "Katy. I need you up here."

"Hi, Katy," he says, and we both laugh.

"Okay, so show me that broken pipe and I'll take care of it and be on my way. From all the good things I'm smelling, I'd say you're having a party tonight."

Upstairs, Angela's rescued the mushrooms from the oven and has the rest of the food ready for warming. "I have to go," she says, "will you be okay with all this?"

"As long as Mark gets the bathroom working again, it'll be fine," I tell her.

"Wow," she says, "first name basis already, huh?" I know she'd like nothing better than for me to find someone irresistible, even if it is the plumber. "And no wedding ring, either," she tells me. "I looked."

Angela thinks Steven is the biggest mistake I've ever made. "Does he make you feel wonderfully happy?" she asks me. "Does he make you feel as though you want to dance? As though you could float straight to him when he's across the room?"

She doesn't expect an answer, but if I had to give her one, it would be 'no.' Because those feelings only happen in movies. Or in daydreams. Never in real life.

***

When Steven arrives, Mark is coming out of the bathroom and I'm still in my robe. The two of them stare at each other for a second. Then I explain.

"It doesn't matter," Steven says, as long as everything's back together again." Then he looks at Mark. "Is it all back together?"

Mark nods. "It'll hold."

"Good," Steven says, then he looks at me. "People will be arriving any second and you're not even dressed yet. You know how important this is, Kathryn. I thought I could count on you."

Mark's putting tools into a box. He stands up, and as he walks past Steven he says, "If it's so important, why aren't you giving her some help?" which leaves Steven speechless and takes my breath away a little, too. He turns to me. "I fixed it, but the pipes are old and need to be replaced. Don't wait too long on that, okay?" He starts to leave, then turns back. "Hope you get back on that bike," he says, gives me a wonderful smile, and then he's gone.

"Who does he think he is," Steven says.

"He's the plumber," I tell him. "And if it weren't for him, your precious party would be floating out the door right now."

"We'll talk about this later," he says. And then the doorbell rings. "And for heaven's sake, get dressed!"

I put on my short black sheath. The one Steven specifically asked me not to wear tonight. I slip on my heels. I go into the bathroom to fix my hair. Sitting on the sink is Mark's business card, a number scrawled across the bottom in pencil.

For the next three hours I pass trays and refill drinks and talk to people I don't really know. It doesn't feel like a party. It feels like a chore. And I keep looking at the clock to see how long until it's over.

Then, once it is, things go from bad to worse. "How could you put those mushrooms out?" Steven says, after the last guest is gone. "They were overcooked."

"Well," I say, "if that's the worst thing that happened to *you* tonight, I wouldn't complain. And you know, Steven ... I really don't want you staying overnight. In fact, I think you should go home and not come back at all." I twist the engagement ring off my finger and hand it to him. "I'm sorry, but you just don't make me happy."

***

A month goes by. Steven doesn't call. And although sometimes I feel a little sad, it doesn't take long for me to start feeling happy again. I get my bike out of the basement and start taking long rides on the weekends. And I keep eyeing the business card Mark left, until finally I call the number. Not the one he scrawled at the bottom, but the official one printed on the card. After all, he did say I needed to replace those pipes.

"Mark?" the woman who answers the phone says.

"Yes," I tell her. "He was out here several weeks ago and fixed a broken pipe. It was a Saturday night."

"Oh," she says. "You must mean Mark Rawlings. He came out and fixed your plumbing?" She laughs a little. "Mr. Rawlings owns the company. I didn't think he did that kind of thing anymore. But I can have someone come out and give you a quote, if you'd like."

I tell her I'll think about it. Which I do for about a minute after I hang up. Then I call the number he wrote on the card.

I smile when I hear his voice. "You probably don't remember me," I say.

"Oh I remember you, Katy," he says. "Did you decide to replace those pipes?"

"Well, eventually," I tell him. "But actually I was wondering if you might like to take a bike ride sometime. My bike's all dusted off and I'm looking for people who like to do what I like to do."

"How about Saturday?" he says. "Eight a.m.? We could meet at your place."

"I'll make us a lunch to bring along," I tell him.

"No," he says. "Let me do that, I make a dynamite chicken salad."

"See you soon then," I tell him. And after I hang up, it happens. For the first time ever, I feel like dancing. Like I could float right across the room.

———

PERFECT TIMING

I look up to find Mac standing in the living room doorway wearing his funny faded fishing hat and holding his fishing gear, and staring at me as if maybe I'll break in two right there in front of him.

"There's no cell service up there, Chrissie," he says. "I just remembered that. What if you need to get hold of me?"

"Will you stop?" I say. "I'll be fine. The baby's not due for two whole weeks. And you'll be back in four days."

This is a trip Mac and three of his friends planned early in the year. Before I got pregnant. It's a trip they used to make every year, and now every other year because there are wives and babies in their lives that make things much more complicated. Mac said he wasn't going this year. I said he was. Because there used to be six friends and now there are only three, and every time they go, someone has to drop out due to family and work commitments. "You have to go," I told him. "This trip gets harder to pull off every time. I want you to go while you can. I know you love it, so just go and have a good time!"

That was me being practical, reasonable, and logical. The way I used to be before I got pregnant. Now I have to fake being all those things, because I haven't really felt practical or logical in eight-and-a-half months. Secretly, it makes me happy that he doesn't want to go. And if I'm totally honest, I suppose I wish he'd just say he absolutely was *not* going and absolutely refuse to let me talk him out of it.

What I really want right now is for Mac to sit down beside me and hold my hand for the next two weeks. I want him to turn to me every fifteen seconds and ask me questions like: "Are you okay?" and "Can I get you anything?"

But the reality is that, mostly thanks to me, Mac is going and I'm pretending to be perfectly happy about it.

He stands there wearing his funny fishing hat, then he comes over and puts his arms around me. "Who's going to rub your back for you tonight?" he asks.

The thought of going to bed without him to snuggle against makes my throat ache, but I won't let him see that. "Don't worry," I say, forcing a smile, "I'll just give that nice guy next door a call."

He gives me a squeeze, and when he lets go, I keep my face buried against his shirt, because I'm afraid my eyes are filling up and if he sees me like that, the trip will be off and he'll get no vacation this year whatsoever.

His comforting arms encircle me again and we stand there holding on to each other until I get myself back under control. Then he gives me a hard, fast kiss. ""Four short days," he whispers in my ear. I follow him to the door and watch him drive off, waving until he's out of sight.

In the kitchen, it's so quiet, I can hear the clock ticking, and although I know it's totally unreasonable, I begin to get mad. Mad at Mac for leaving, for not seeing that I really didn't want him to go after all, for doing exactly what I kept urging him to do, for doing a perfectly reasonable and practical thing.

I head for the refrigerator and the half-dozen brownies left over from last night's dessert. A contraction catches me just as I'm opening the door. I've been having them for about a week now, random contractions. "Nothing to worry about," the doctor tells me, "just part of the normal process. They have nothing to do with actual labor."

I put two brownies on a plate, even though I just had breakfast half an hour ago, and put some water on for tea. And while I'm waiting for the water to boil, I eat six whole-wheat crackers and a handful of raisins. Then I decide that the only way to get myself to stop eating is to get out of the kitchen and go to work. Officially, my maternity leave doesn't start for another ten days, but I have a boss who doesn't care where the accounting gets handled, just as long as the figures add up. So I've been working from my den for the past two weeks, and that's where I head with my tea and my brownies.

I turn on my computer and work until eleven. That's when I get another contraction and then another one ten minutes later. I stretch out on the couch. "Okay now, baby," I say "this is not a good time for you to be doing this. So I suggest you change any plans you might have and wait until your daddy gets back." And then, for absolutely no good reason except that I'm feeling very sorry for myself, I start to cry, and try not to think about Mac and how he's abandoned me at what may turn out to be the most important moment of our life.

But then the contractions stop and before I know it, it's two o'clock and I've been sound asleep for three hours. There's a text on my phone from Mac. It says, *signing off now. Service fading. See you soon! All my love.*

I lie there for a while and think about the baby. We don't know if it's a girl or a boy, so we have two names … Hayden, after Mac's grandfather, and Skye, because we both love it. Hayden or Skye's room is all ready. The walls are sunny yellow, the crib is white. There are blankets and onesies and tiny little gowns. And while I remind myself to choose a mobile for over the crib, and do it soon, I get a contraction that's different. Just different.

When I call my doctor, I tell her that the contractions started over an hour ago. "They're coming every seven or eight minutes," I tell her. "And they're not stopping."

"It could still be false labor," she tells me. "When they start coming every five minutes, then go to the hospital. Until then, lie down and relax."

"Relax," I mutter to myself. I go upstairs to pack a bag, just in case, look at our wedding photo atop the bureau. "Some husband you are," I tell the picture. "Here I am about to give birth to our firstborn and you're probably standing in water up to your knees, reeling in your first catch of the day." I paw through my closet for my overnighter, but it's not there. And then I remember where it is. It's with Mac up at Rainbow Lake, full of cans of beans and soup.

I grab a Lord & Taylor shopping bag and throw in anything I think I might need, but it takes a while, because I have to keep stopping every time I have a contraction. "Seven minutes," I say to myself, "six minutes. Oh my god."

I call Mac's brother at work and tell him it's time and that Mac left for Rainbow Lake almost eight hours ago.

"He went fishing?" he says. "I'll be there in fifteen minutes."

"No," I tell him. "I can get myself to the hospital. I just want you to try and get hold of Mac. There's no cell service up there, but can you try to call in and have somebody find him?"

"I'll do it," he says. "Even if I have to drive up and bring him back myself."

I think about the trip to the hospital and decide that if I time it right, I can probably get to the ER with only one contraction. I brush my teeth, and when I look at myself in the mirror, it hits me for the first time, really *hits* me. Mac is going to miss it. And it doesn't matter so much that he's not going to be there to hold my hand and put a cool cloth against my forehead. Or that he's not going to be there to rub my back and tell me to push. What really matters is that he's not going to be there to see our son or our daughter born. He's not going to get to hold the baby or sing the silly little songs he's been crooning into my stomach. He won't see the baby until it's hours old

Tears make my reflection go all wavy, and I bite my lip to make them go away. Then another contraction takes my mind off everything for a while, and I realize that although they're not necessarily getting closer, each one is lasting longer and longer.

I grab my Lord & Taylor bag, hold on tight to the railing all the way down the stairs, and take the car keys off the hook in the kitchen. I open the door and walk straight into Mac.

I stare at him for a few perplexed seconds. "What are you doing here?" I demand, surprised at my tone.

He frowns. "Why? Is the guy next door here?" Then he smiles and cups my face with his hands. "I'm here because I got halfway there and all I could think about was what the heck I was doing *there* when the two most important people in my life were *here*. So I emptied the bait box, hung a U-turn, and broke speed limits all the way home."

"You have no idea how glad I am to see you," I say. And then I remember his brother Neil, who's probably driving up there right this minute to get Mac. "Your brother, oh no ... he's on his way to get you."

"Get me? Why?"

That's when I have the hardest contraction yet. I squeeze Mac's shirt with both hands. "Because it's happening! The baby's coming!"

"The baby? Now?"

I nod through the rest of the contraction, watching Mac's face go from confused to worried to completely disbelieving. I take a deep breath. "I was just leaving to go to the hospital." Then, "Five minutes," I tell him. "That one was just five minutes. We gotta go!"

He slides me into the front seat. He's still wearing his fishing hat.

"My bag," I tell him. "I need my bag."

He runs off, comes back with the overnighter and throws it into the back seat.

"Are you sure you're okay?" he asks at least fifteen times on the way to the hospital.

I nod. I pant. I hold his hand, which is big and warm and full of strength in case I run out of my own. "Everything's fine," I say, between contractions," just fine." I want to tell him other things, too. That the reason everything's fine is because he's here and we're going to do this together. That his coming home means everything in the world. That he's going to be the best daddy there ever was. That he's already the best husband.

I also want to tell him that he'll need to bring the beans and soup back home and get the stuff out of the Lord & Taylor bag still sitting in the kitchen. But that can wait. Because right now, we have more important business to take care of.

———

WHAT'S IN A NAME?

Behind me, Ellie's computer keys stop clicking. Her chair creaks and she makes a sound — "Mmmmmm..." as though what she's looking at is extremely interesting and something she wants to share.

But I've been in a bad mood now for eight days, ever since Dan sent me his 'It's been fun but let's just be friends' text. So I ignore Ellie, and finally, she pushes her chair into mine, almost hard enough to give me whiplash.

"For Pete's sake!" I say. I point to my computer screen, which is now filled with eights. "Look what you made me do!"

"Oh, Morgan, don't be such a grouch," she says. She points to an X8oZ form on her screen. "Just up from Personnel," she says. "New guy. And get this name: *Chase*."

"So?" I say.

"I like it," she says. Then she closes her eyes. "He's six-two, works out, and lives in a studio apartment with two skylights."

"You really expect me to believe that all that information is on his X8oZ?"

"It's the name," she says. "It's what it conjures up."

"Baloney," I say.

"Oh Morgan ... you've lost your imagination. Not to mention your sense of the possible."

"Yes," I tell her. "I lost it exactly eight days ago and have no intention of getting any of it back."

"He's in the art department," Ellie continues, ignoring me, "which means he's creative and intuitive. Plus, he's single — and I happen to think there's a lot in a name."

"Maybe there is if you choose it yourself after you reach the age of thirty."

She shakes her head. "It helps to form your personality. I mean, you can bet a guy named Chase isn't going to show up wearing a backwards baseball cap or have empty beer cans rolling around in his car. And anyway, look at *you*. I'd give anything to have your name."

"It's the name of a horse," I say.

"A *thoroughbred*."

"Then I supposed you don't know that Cary Grant's real name was Archibald. Or that John Wayne's first name was Marion." But she just stares at me because she has no idea what I'm talking about. I love old movies and old movie stars, but Ellie doesn't even know that there were other James Bonds before Daniel Craig.

She stands up. "I want to get a look at this guy. C'mon. Let's visit the art department."

"Not on your life," I tell her. "I've given up on looks, names, and biceps. From now on I want someone…" I pause, searching for exactly what it is I want, "…mature."

She frowns. "Old?"

"Not old. Mature. Someone who's responsible and empathetic. Not someone who's so childish and gutless that he breaks up with me in a text!"

"Yeah," she says, sitting down again. "That was completely crummy."

At 10:30, she bangs the back of my chair again, but not so hard this time. "Coffee break," she says. "Let's take a walk."

I know we're going to end up in the art department, where, I hope, Ellie will find that her fantasy man is four-foot-eight, toothless, and hasn't understood a joke since sixth grade.

We stop at the entrance and stand there trying to look nonchalant. I recognize everyone except a bespectacled guy in the far corner with wispy red hair and slumped shoulders.

"I told you," I say.

"Maybe that's not him," she says.

"It might be a whole lot better if it is. I mean, you just can't go around picking boyfriends using the same methods we used when we were sixteen. Maybe it's time we both grew up. I mean, think about it Ellie. Dan was gorgeous, right? And he was about as sensitive as an armadillo. And then there was your Tony and all those muscles, especially the ones between his ears. And my Sam with his big ego. And don't forget Chris, with that Corvette, which he'll love better than any woman who ever gets to sit in it."

"All right," she grumbles. "I get your point."

We take one more look around. "It's for your own good," I tell her. "The best thing this Chase guy could turn out to be is short, pale, and as near-sighted as an old goat." Then I giggle a little and turn to leave, and walk smack into someone's chest.

"Excuse me," he says, "I just need to get through."

"Oh, right," I say. "Sorry. We didn't mean to block the …"

"Hey Chase," someone calls out, "a fax just came in for you. It's marked URGENT.

"I'm on it," Chase says, and then he looks straight at me and points to his eyes. "Twenty-twenty," he says.

Ellie pulls me out into the hallway. Neither of us says a word until we're back in our office.

"Oh my god," Ellie says, recovering her voice, "did you *see* him?"

I roll my eyes. As if I could have missed him.

"Six-two at least," she says.

I look at her. "And at this very moment," I say, "he's thinking that he just met the two most brainless women in the world."

"Yeah." She sighs. "I guess you blew it, huh?"

I could remind her whose idea going down there was in the first place, but I don't. Because right now, all I want to do is forget that the whole thing even happened. And most of all, I want to forget those amused, twenty-twenty blue eyes.

Except I can't. I can't stop thinking about how I felt when I realized who he was. I can't stop feeling embarrassed that he was standing right behind me listening to every word I said. And I can't stop remembering how it felt when I walked into him, the smell of his aftershave, his smile, the way his hair curled just on the edge of his collar.

I keep telling myself these are not the things that matter to me anymore — smiles and eyes and broad shoulders. But I just can't forget them.

***

"So I guess you're going to eat lunch at your desk for the rest of eternity?" Ellie asks.

"I happen to *like* eating lunch at my desk," I tell her.

"It's ridiculous," she says. "We haven't gone out in a week. I suppose next you'll start wearing a bag over your head in case you run into him in the revolving doors at the end of the day."

"I have no idea what you're talking about. Run into whom?"

"Oh, c'mon, Morgan. It was just an odd little incident. And I bet he's already forgotten about it."

"Listen, I'll go out with you to lunch tomorrow, all right? Just to prove that what happened isn't bothering me in the least."

She looks at me for a second, then nods.

I take a bite of my cheese sandwich after she leaves. It's not just what happened last week in the art department doorway, it's everything that's been happening for the last couple of years. It's Dan and Josh and half a dozen other guys who started out as Prince Charmings, then turned into frogs right before my eyes. And if all the things that attract me to someone in the first place turn out to be illusions, how will I ever trust my feelings or my instincts ever?

That's when Chase walks in. He looks around, then sees me staring at him. "There you are," he says, "I was beginning to think you were an apparition. "But I kept seeing your friend, Ellie, so I figured you must be real, too." He sits down. "I guess you know my name," he says, "but I don't know yours."

I swallow. "Morgan."

"I hate bad beginnings," he says. "I'm hoping we can do it over. Get to know each other the right way."

Then he smiles, and I feel my instincts getting into gear. I have to fight hard to put them back into neutral.

"I'm not usually such a jerk," he says. "I mean with that twenty-twenty stuff."

"Oh, no" I say. "You had every right ... and I should be the one to apologize to you. It's just that...." I stop. I shrug. "It would take a while to explain."

He looks at my sandwich. "Maybe we could go someplace and talk? Grab a couple of desserts?"

I feel all my untrustworthy senses telling me to go for it, which makes me certain I should say no. But then it hits me — that he's come looking for me. That he's faced a situation I was trying to avoid. That he's apologized for something that wasn't his fault. And I know what it takes to do those kinds of things. It takes maturity.

I wrap up my sandwich and decide to let all my instincts come flying out of neutral. "We could go to *Delights*," I say.

"*Delights*." He stands up and holds out one hand. "Now, how could we possibly go wrong," he says, "with a name like that?"

———

FALLING

I watch Connor rushing up the driveway as the school bus pulls away. The back door opens, then closes with a bang, and Connor invades the kitchen. "Can we go see him?" he asks.

I pick up the fruit basket all ready to go on the counter. "Let's do it."

Almost every day since we moved here, Connor's spent afternoons with his new best friend, Mr. Keene. They've built a cuckoo clock and half a catapult. Connor's learned to make a kite and hoot like an owl. Mr. Keene is a friend and grandfather rolled into one. At least until the heart attack.

The woman who opens the door is new. There has been a parade of caregivers since he came home from the hospital, all of them, not surprisingly, resistant to having an eight-year-old visitor in their way. So the only time Connor gets to see Mr. Keene now is the one day a week I work from home. And sometimes on a Sunday. It was a serious heart attack, and Mr. Keene doesn't have the energy he once had for Connor. Barely has the energy to make it through a one-hour visit. Still, I see concern in the old man's eyes, not for himself, but for us. For the little family he decided to 'take under his wing.' And I do my best to let him know we're okay. That we miss him, that Connor misses him especially, but that he doesn't need to worry about a leaky faucet or a loose shingle on our roof, or 'pass along' a six-pound roast beef 'a friend' gave him for nothing and that he can't eat all by himself, when I know very well he bought it for us. He's really the best friend Connor and I have had in a long time, and I'll hold on to all his kindnesses for as long as I live.

"Just a half-hour today," caregiver Nancy tells us, and I can see as soon as we sit down that he's not feeling well. I let Connor tell him every important thing that's happened since Sunday, and Mr. Keene listens with his eyes closed and a smile on his face. But after a while, even Connor seems to realize that maybe the best thing is for us to go so he can rest.

"We'll be back," Connor says, leaning close, and Mr. Keene opens his eyes, raises one hand, and touches Connor's cheek. "We'll finish the catapult when you're better," Connor says, and tears spring to my eyes.

I pat Mr. Keene's arm. "You take care of yourself," I tell him. "We both miss you."

"I worry about you," he says.

I lean close to him. "No, please don't. We're fine. You've helped Connor so much. He loves you. We both do."

The next day, we notice a blue car in Mr. Keene's driveway. A caretaker comes in the morning and leaves in the evening, but the blue car stays all night long.

"It might be Mr. Keene's daughter," I tell Connor. "Remember the picture on his mantle of his grandson, Nicky? I bet Nicky's mother has come to take care of her father."

"He'll get better now," Connor says. "She'll make him better."

When Sunday comes, we walk over to the house, but it's not a woman who answers the door; it's a man. A man who looks so familiar, I feel happy to see him. Even though I have no idea who he is. "Connor?" he says, "hey, buddy, we've been waiting for you." And then he looks at me. "And Connor's mom. Is it Kim?" I nod. "Hi," he says, "I'm Nick Keene. Please come in. Gramps talks about you two all the time."

Connor's eyes are big. He stands there staring at Mr. Keene's grandson. And I guess I do, too, because the grandson named Nick in the mantelpiece photo is about thirteen.

"Are you the world traveler?" Connor asks.

Nick chuckles. "That's what he calls me, all right."

"Connor?" Mr. Keene calls out, "what's taking you so long to get in here?" The sound of his voice, so much stronger than just a few days ago, surprises me enough to step through the door.

"Grandad showed me the catapult you two are building," Nick says to Connor. "That's quite a machine."

"We're going to catapult a giant box full of popcorn," Connor says.

Nick laughs.

Mr. Keene isn't in bed. He's sitting up in the living room, looking so much better than he did the last time. He puts his arms out and I give him a hug. "You're back to yourself!" I say.

"Oh, some mix-up with the medications," he tells me. "Have to admit that for a while there I thought the end was near."

"That'll be the day you go down without a fight," Nick says. Then he looks at me, a look that says, yes, his grandfather is better, but not all better. Not yet.

"I still get tired just sitting," Mr. Keene says. "It's going to take a little while yet. But I bet Nick would be happy to take over finishing that catapult, Connor. That okay with you?"

"Will you?" Connor asks Nick. "And will you tell me about the Gobi Desert and how to find a meteorite?"

Nick looks at me. "Sure will. If it's okay with your mom."

I feel strangely torn, wanting to say *yes, of course* but afraid to. "Well..." I look at Connor, his face full of expectation, "...maybe in a week or so. But right now, I think Nick and Mr. Keene have their hands full."

"A week?" Connor says. He makes it sound like a lifetime.

"Whenever your mom says," Nick tells him. I plan to be around for a while." He smiles at me. "Long as it takes to get Grandad back on his feet."

Connor is clearly disappointed. All weekend he tells me the stories Mr. Keene told him about Nick in Patagonia, Nick in the

Sahara, Nick in the Galapagos. Nick has clearly become Connor's idol, and I am clearly standing between the two of them. And Connor can't quite figure out why.

Frankly, neither can I. But Connor also knows he's the man of our house and that he has certain responsibilities. Cleaning out the basement takes three afternoons. The garage, another two.

"It's almost a week," he says at dinner. "Can I visit Mr. Keene and Nick tomorrow?"

"I need your help with my storyboard," I tell him. "This is a very important job, so I really need you."

"I guess," he sighs.

But the next day, neither of us can concentrate. We keep glancing outside, at Nick in his back yard taking pictures of something on the ground.

Connor looks at me.

"Okay," I say. "But be polite and don't...."

He's gone before I can finish. And finally, my own curiosity wins out.

"It's a snake that's swallowing a toad, Mom! Look!"

"A garter snake," Nick says. "Harmless." Then he looks up at me and smiles. "Unless you're a toad."

"Nick saw an Anaconda swallow a whole deer!" Connor says.

Nick looks at me, shrugs. "Mostly I wait around with my camera until something starts to happen," he says, "and then I press my auto shoot and hope I get something that's view-worthy." Looking at him, I get a feeling I thought I was over. "I'm ... uh ..." I stammer, "I'm going to see your..." And then I flee.

Inside, Mr. Keene's resting with his eyes closed, and I start to tiptoe away.

"Don't go," he says.

"The two of them are out there watching a snake," I tell him.

He nods. "Nick was watching snakes before he could walk. And once he could walk, he was always disappearing."

"A world traveler," I say. "I knew one once."

"But yours took off and never came back," he says.

I nod.

He points to a bowl of apples on the table. "What a shame," he says, "to judge all apples because the first one you bite into is bad. And that one out there … well, even if he weren't my grandson, I'd vouch that he's not one of the bad ones."

Connor sees me watching from the doorway. "Nick says there's a reptile zoo. He says you and me should go. Can we, Mom?"

I glance at Mr. Keene. I think about what might have happened to him if he'd just accepted the way he felt when he came home, if the mixed-up medicines had never been replaced.

"Sure," I tell Connor, "we can go. But maybe Nick could come along, too? I bet he could answer all your questions a lot better than I could." I look at Nick. "We could learn a lot."

Nick glances up at me, smiles. "Saturday?"

I nod yes and smile back.

———

A CHANGE OF HEART

"**Well**, if you ask me," Olivia says, "you both need your oil changed." And then she stares me down. Olivia is my older sister. Her husband Ben owns the only service station for fourteen miles up and down the coast, which makes them pretty well-off and makes Olivia use a lot of job-related jargon.

"Well, *I'm* the one getting married," I say, "and I guess I have the right to choose anyone I please."

She stares out across the road at the sand dunes. "The only pleasing thing about Andy Fenton is the fact that he works over in Columbia all week and I only have to risk running into him on weekends."

I can feel my neck getting tense, which means she's going to give me a headache if she keeps it up. "How can you say a thing like that?" Usually, it makes me mad, but today, for some reason, I think I'm going to cry. "I would never say a thing like that about Ben. Never."

She turns toward me with that *you are so dumb* look on her face, which I have had to deal with ever since I can remember. "That's because Ben is a sweet, gentle, down-to-earth guy, and Andy Fenton is a jerk."

I jump up. "That's it. If you think I'm going to sit here and listen to you say terrible things about the man I'm going to marry, you are one hundred percent mistaken." I start down the porch steps determined to not let her see me cry.

"If you loved him," she calls after me, "That would be different. But you don't and you know it."

I'm on the sidewalk now, walking fast, the road, and the grass and the air all blurry through my tears. Sometimes I hate

Olivia. I hate her because sometimes I feel she can see right into my soul. See what I'm thinking—even when I don't want to see it myself. I turn down our road, walk right past our driveway and have to turn around and go back. Lately I've been doing things like that ... forgetting to call the wedding photographer, showing up for the blood test a day late, leaving the engraved thank-you notes Mama insisted on buying under my chair at the luncheonette.

Mama smiles and says everyone in love acts like that. Daddy says Andy will be lucky if I show up at the right church. Olivia sniffs and tells me I'm making Freudian slips. That people only forget to do the things they subconsciously don't want to do in the first place. She makes me so mad.

What Olivia would like is to see me ruin my life and marry Brian. She doesn't seem to realize Brian was just a phase I went through when I still believed that living someone meant you had to feel it all the way down to your toes. What she doesn't realize is that loving someone that way sets you up for the most excruciating sort of heartache. And thanks to Brian Jessup, I've had enough heartache to last me three lifetimes.

I go inside, walk through the dining room on my way upstairs. There are three new packages sitting on the table, next to all the other wedding gifts. I look at the crystal, the silver bowls, the china—all these things that belong to me and don't feel as though they belong to me at all. I decide not to open the new ones and go on up to my room.

Although I know I'm supposed to do something this afternoon, I can't remember what it is. I walk from my door to the window, look out, go to my bureau, go back to the window, go over and sit on the bed, get up and go back to the bureau. Taking a week off from work before the wedding is driving me crazy. I should have stayed at the bank until the last minute. Then there would be less time to think. The thank-you cards Mama rescued from the luncheonette are sitting on the bureau. *Mr. and Mrs. Andrew Fenton.* That's me. Mrs. Andrew Fenton. Mrs. Fenton. Jessica Fenton. Jessie Fenton.

I turn around and go sit on my bed. No matter what Olivia says, I'm absolutely positive that getting Brian Jessup out of my life has saved me from a peck of misery. It has also saved me from being Jessica Jessup.

I lie down and stare up at the ceiling, and hope all the petals on Brian's mother's prize roses fall off. She deserves it for being such a nag. *Now Jessica, dear … you and Brian have been so close for so long … and well, do you think it's wise? After all, you can't expect to choose the right dessert if you haven't sampled all of them, at least a little. Now, can you?*

No one had to draw me a picture. I knew it wasn't me she was so worried for. It was Brian. Mrs. Jessup liked me as well as anybody up until the time Brian began buying me ice cream sodas after school. That's when Mrs. Jessup started watching me. I could feel it. She started finding all kinds of things wrong with me. I could feel that, too. And what she was really saying with all her *Jessie, dears* was that I was by far the poorest dessert on her Brian's tray and she fully intended to do as much as she could to get him to try all the others.

I still can't believe he gave in. "Just for a few months, Jessie," he said, "to get her off our backs, and it's not going to make any difference, right? I love you, Jessie. I always have and I always will."

"You always will, Brian Jessup," I say to the ceiling. "At least until Nicole Perry jumped up on your dessert tray." I decide to think about something else and stop wasting my valuable time. Then I hear Olivia and Mama talking downstairs in the dining room. "Well, if you ask me…" Olivia is saying. She looks up when I walk in and she stops in mid-sentence.

"Jessie," Mama says, "where did you come from? I didn't hear you come in. How was the dress?"

"Dress?"

"Does it need more fitting?"

That was it. What I was supposed to do this afternoon. Mama's eyes get big. "Don't tell me you forgot. How could you forget? It's your wedding dress!"

Olivia gives Mama a meaningful look, then she taps one of the unopened packages on the table. "You could have opened them," I tell her.

"But *I'm* not the excited bride," she says. No one knows how to be sarcastic better than Olivia.

"Open them, honey," Mama says.

The first gift is from Mrs. Bean. She lives down the street with her cats. Seventeen of them. Her gift is a ceramic cat. Everyone in town who gets married has a ceramic cat from Mrs. Bean in a box in their attic. The second box is full of tissue paper that I keep pulling our and pulling out. "It's a joke," I say, "just a box full of paper." But at the bottom is something round, and when I unwrap it, I have a hard time keeping my face from showing anything.

"How pretty," Mama says. "What is it? Who's it from?"

"It's a geode," I say, and search through the tissue, pretending to look for a card. I search several minutes, because it give me time to collect myself. "No card," I say. "Guess whoever sent it forgot."

Mama takes the geode out of my hand and holds it up, turns it so the light catches the crystals inside. "It's the prettiest thing," she says. "What's a geode?"

"A kind of rock," I tell her.

"Wasn't that Brian's hobby?" Olivia asks. "Rocks? Didn't you two go off rock-hunting all the time?"

I clap my hand against my forehead. "I just remembered that Luanne is waiting for me to perm her hair. Gotta go."

"Supper's in an hour and a half," Mama says. "Are you going to have time to do her hair and get back here by six-thirty? It's Thursday, you know."

Andy comes to dinner every Thursday. He'd like to come more often because he says he dreams about Mama's cooking, but I won't let him come more than one night because all anyone does is sit around and talk wedding, wedding, wedding until I could scream. And I'm afraid that one of these Thursdays, after Andy's licked his plate clean of chicken and biscuits and gravy, and congratulated himself yet again on catching Mama's daughter, I'm going to look him straight in the eye ad tell him that the only thing I've ever cooked in my life is Quaker oatmeal—and it was lumpy.

"It won't matter if I'm late," I tell her. "All he's after is your gravy." And then I run out the door and start walking fast toward Luanne's. But when I get to her house, I keep going. Past all the houses, down the dirt path into the woods until I can see the salt pond and the cliff above it. It's been my quiet place since I was just a kid. Where I went when I got yelled at or when I was lonely or when Brian and I had a fight. It's where I went when I found out about Brian and Nicole and where I came after Andy said, "Hey, let's get married," and I said, "Sure, why not?"

I climb up to the top and sit down. Everything was going just fine. And then Brian Jessup had to go and send me a rock. *A few month can't hurt us, Jessie*. That's what he said so many times he got me believing it, too. And there I was, starting my new job at the bank and he was going off to school. *We're going to be a hundred miles apart, anyway. So why should you sit home every night?*

I guess I was supposed to say, *why should you sit home every night, too*, but I didn't. Because that's what I wanted. Him sitting home every night. "I'll write every day," he said, "and call once a week. And anyway, I'll be home at Christmas."

But the two of us never made it to Christmas.

And I still don't know why I went to that dance in Larchmont. I didn't want to go. Those dances were always tacky. But Luanne kept acting as if she was going to die if I didn't go with her. And I was getting tired of listening to the girls at the bank every Monday morning talking about what they did over the weekend and who they saw and who they wished they'd seen, when all I was doing was sitting home waiting for the phone to ring. And to think I felt bad about going while Brian was sitting in a library studying about rocks.

I really hope I will never be that dumb again in my entire life.

My stomach still gets tight when I think about seeing him there. Especially when I think about seeing there with Nicole Perry hanging all over him. Maybe if he'd acted annoyed by her, I could have forgiven him. But he was smiling and his arm seemed glued around her shoulders. He wasn't studying geology in the library. He hadn't even told me he was home for the weekend. He was having a good time with a girl who'd been named Miss Orange County two years in a row.

"You can't spend the whole night in the ladies' room," Luanne told me.

"I intend to spend the rest of my life here," I told her.

"It's not like you two were engaged," she said. "I mean, you both agreed to see other people, right?"

"The thing is," I said, "he's seeing Nicole and I'm seeing you."

"Well, Andy Fenton is over at the refreshment booth," she said, "and everyone knows he's been in love with you forever. And isn't he better than sitting *here* all night?"

When I walked over to Andy, he acted as though he knew it was going to happen eventually. That loving me for as long as he had would make me love him back some day. And when Brian saw us dancing, me smiling as though I was having the time of my life, it almost made me genuinely happy to see the look of complete disbelief on his face as he tried to disentangle himself from Miss Orange County.

"What are you doing here?" Brian said, ignoring Andy as if he wasn't even there.

"Same as you," I answered, with my best friendly smile pasted across my face. "Going out. Having a good time. Sampling." And then I danced Andy away and spent the rest of the night convincing myself that the significant change of heart Andy had always expected from me was real.

Brian called ten times before I finally talked to him. And then I only did it because Mama refused to make up another excuse.

"Why are you doing this," he said.

"I decided to practice what you preached," I told him. "And although I had doubts at first, I finally saw how right you were. I'm having fun. And I'm glad to see you are, too." Although that last part almost choked me.

"But, Jessie … Nicole isn't …"

"She's a doll," I said, cutting him short. "You make a cute couple. And Brian … if it weren't for you, I'd never have gotten to know Andy, and he's coming up the walk this very minute, so I have to go. You have fun and maybe we'll see each other real soon. Bye."

I climb down from the cliff and walk home. I've been here long enough so they're probably on second helpings of chicken and gravy by now.

***

The next morning Olivia calls and wakes me up at seven o'clock. "You've got to do me a favor," she says.

"I'm busy," I tell her.

"I'm supposed to be at a property I'm trying to sell at nine," she says, ignoring me, "and I can't make it. You have to do it for me. Someone's going to be there at nine to test the well. All you have to do is be there, watch them do it, and go home. Is that too much to ask?"

"Yes, it is, but I'll do it anyway."

The house turns out to be on the other side of the bay. Way out on a wing of land. A summer place set high on piers so storm tides can't hurt it. I walk around and peer in the windows to pass the time. Pretty soon a van comes down the road. It's a white van with a drop of blue water painted on its side. It stops, and Brian gets out. Everything about him is familiar. The way he shifts his weight to his right leg, hooks his thumbs in his belt, smiles his slow smile. His eyes are even bluer than I remember.

"I didn't know it was going to be you," I say, once my brain recovers from the shock. Why, I wonder, did I have to have Olivia for a sister.

"Well, I didn't know it was going to be you, either," he says. He points a thumb at the van. "Summer job til school starts again."

"How nice," I say. We stare at each other. Then I look at my watch. "Is this going to take long?"

For a second he looks at me as though he's forgotten why he's here. Then he shakes his head. "No, takes hardly any time at all."

"Good," I say.

He gets the key from under the porch steps and we go inside. When he goes to turn on the main water valve, the handle is missing, and by the time he finds the right handle in his van and attaches it, turns on the water and lets it run long enough to clear the pipes, takes the sample he needs and then tests the water pressure and the intake rate, it's almost noon. "So that's your idea of hardly any time at all?" I ask.

He heads for his van, stops, turns around and stands there for a second. "Have a nice wedding," he says.

It'll be the way I'll always remember him, standing there ten feet away, a whole world between us.

I drive off, take the first curve in the road too fast, and then almost can't stop in time. I sit there staring at the swirling water that's now connecting the two marshes on either side of the road. And then Brian pulls up and stops behind me.

"What the heck…" He looks at the water, whistles. "It's a tideway, for Pete's sake. Why didn't someone say something?"

"A tideway? You mean we're cut off until the tide goes out? We're stuck here for *twelve* hours?"

"Unless you think you know exactly where the road is and don't mind driving into a salt marsh if you're wrong."

As we drive back to the house, I try calling Olivia, but she's not picking up.

"You don't have to act like it's the end of the world," Brian says, sitting down on the porch steps. "I have other things I'm supposed to be doing, too. And when I called into work to tell them just now, Joe sounded like he was two seconds away from firing me."

"I'm so sad for you," I say, sitting down beside him.

"Funny, isn't it?" he says, after a while. "How things turn out? I mean, there's Andy Fenton following you around all those years, and you jut ignoring him. And then..." He snaps his fingers. "Just like that you find out he's the one you really wanted all along."

"All along," I say.

He bends over, picks up a handful of grass, throws it down. "What do I have to do to get you to talk to me?"

"Isn't that what we're doing?"

"Okay," he says, mad now. "All you have to do is one thing. Tell me you love Andy Fenton more than you ever loved me and I'll leave you alone and spend the next twelve hours in the van."

I try. I try really hard, but I just can't.

"Then why are you doing this?" he finally says. "Why are you doing this to us?"

"Me?" What I want to do is give him a really good shove, but I control myself. "*You're* the one who stopped communicating. *You're* the one who showed up at that dance with Nicole Perry. *You're* the one who did this to us. *You*, Brian. Not me!"

"Damn it, Jessie. That's not fair. You were at that dance, too. You were there with Andy."

"No I wasn't. I was there with Luanne. Andy Fenton was just a convenient way for me to save some of my pride."

He stares at me. "Okay. I did go out with some other girls. But the only reason I did it was because you were already seeing other guys even before my first week of classes was over."

"Seeing other guys? What guys? Who told you that?"

"My mother. She said it just showed that our breaking up was the best thing for both of us."

"Your mother said that?" I stare at the line of the ocean shining in the noon sun. So now it isn't just a matter of setting the record straight, it's a matter of handling this without starting a family feud.

"At least I didn't decide to marry any of those girls," he says. He looks at me, his eyes full of hurt. "Because I never even came close to loving even one of them. Not the way I loved you."

"Does that mean you don't anymore?" I ask.

"Don't what?"

"Love me."

We look at each other.

"That's what makes it so hard," he says. "I think I love you even more."

I take a deep breath. "I think we have to be very careful here," I tell him. "Because we have to make sure nobody gets hurt more than they have to. First of all, it was probably a good thing we took a year off. Because it showed us that what we had, what we have, is real. But I'm supposed to be getting married in five days."

"And Andy if going to feel bad," he says. "Because losing you is about the worst feeling in the world. I know."

We sit there leaning against each other. I think about the gifts and the engraved thank-you notes, my wedding dress, all the invitations. I wonder if telling Andy he can keep coming to dinner every Thursday will help. But mostly I think about how much I've missed feeling Brian's arms around me and how I want to keep them there forever.

"Did you get my gift?" he asks.

I nod.

"There's a belief that if you send an amethyst to someone who's gone from you, it will bring them back."

"Then it must be true," I say.

"Jessie," he says, "it should be you and me getting married."

I snuggle against him. I think of all the people I'm going to have to tell. But then I remember that almost all of them just want me to be happy. And I decide that the first person who's going to hear my news is Olivia.

——

BOOKS BY THIS AUTHOR

SHORT STORY COLLECTIONS
AFTERNOON DELIGHT BOOK ONE
AFTERNOON DELIGHT BOOK TWO
AFTERNOON DELIGHT BOOK THREE
AFTERNOON DELIGHT BOOK FOUR
AFTERNOON DELIGHT BOOK FIVE
COW HORMONES

NOVELS
CLICK
DON'T LOOK DOWN
A DANCE WITH THE DEVIL
PAYBACK
LOVE CANAL
RIDDLE
STINKBUG
50 ACRES MORE OR LESS
MOON OF THE DARK RED CALVES

www.ingramcontent.com/pod-product-compliance
Lightning Source LLC
Chambersburg PA
CBHW020639130626
46552CB00003B/1311